Rebel of Dark Creek

Sono
Nis
Press

VICTORIA, BRITISH COLUMBIA

Rebel of Dark Creek
by Nikki Tate

Canadian Cataloguing in Publication Data

Tate, Nikki, 1962-
  Rebel of Dark Creek

  (Stable mates ; 1)
  ISBN 1-55039-076-7
I. Title. II. Series.
PS8589.A8735R42 1997   jC813'.54   C97-910670-2
PZ7.T2113Re 1997

We acknowledge the support of the Canada Council
for the Arts for our publishing program.

Poem and book excerpts from:
Belonging by Sandy Shreve, Sono Nis Press 1997
Horsemanship: A Comprehensive Book on Training The Horse and Its Rider
by Waldemar Seunig,Doubleday & Company Inc., Garden City,
New York, 1956
The Love Song of J. Alfred Prufrock by T.S. Eliot,The Complete Poems
and Plays, Faber and Faber Limited, London, 1969

Cover illustration © 1997 by Pat Cupples

Published by
SONO NIS PRESS
1725 Blanshard Street
Victoria, BC V8W 2J8
http://www.islandnet.com/~sononis/

PRINTED AND BOUND IN CANADA

For Hilary,
the best groom a friend ever had

and for Tramp,
who has gone to sweet feed heaven.

Chapter One

"Are you sure I'm supposed to drop you off at the stables?"

Jessa nodded and held the birthday party invitation in front of her mother.

"Jessa! I can't read when I'm driving!"

Jessa put the invitation in her lap and looked for house numbers on the mailboxes along the narrow country road.

"4660—it must be the next one," she said. "4662 . . ." Jessa read the big brass numbers on the stone gate post. "This must be it."

Jessa's mom pulled into the long driveway.

"Wow! Nice place," she said as they passed beneath the graceful archway made by the branches of an avenue of stately maple trees.

Jessa nodded in agreement. Just beyond the trees, white fences stretched across green pastures which followed the gentle, rolling contours of the land until, just out of sight, the green grass dipped over a rise to meet the sea somewhere below.

"What does her father do for a living?"

Jessa shrugged. "I'm not sure. I know he travels a lot because Rachel always brings souvenirs from his trips to school."

"So, what's with all these horses?"

Jessa looked out the window at several mares grazing under the spreading branches of an old Garry Oak tree. One foal with a white snip playfully tossed its head and darted towards another foal. The second young one reared up as if boxing with its companion. Several other foals nursed or lay sprawled in the long, cool grass.

"I'm not sure, a hobby maybe?" said Jessa. The setting of the Blumen Estate was just about perfect for someone who raised horses.

The rounded, olive green Gulf Islands, and beyond them, the San Juans retreated into the distance before they disappeared into a soft, gray haze which hid the mountains on the far side of the strait.

As they drove slowly through the neatly manicured grounds, Jessa idly stroked the bow on top of the carefully wrapped present which rested on her lap. She thought of the model horse she had chosen for Rachel Blumen's birthday gift. It suddenly seemed to be a pathetic offering. *Why would anyone want a plastic horse when they lived on a gorgeous horse ranch with a whole herd of horses?* Jessa sighed. It was too late now to get out of going to the party.

The long driveway curved around a stand of cedar trees and the view slipped out of sight behind them. Jessa's mom shifted gears and the car back-fired twice before it puttered on. Jessa swallowed hard. She wanted to ask her mom to let her out of the car so she could walk the rest of the way. Getting out of their old beater in full view of Rachel and her friends was so embarrassing.

Jessa looked at her mom who seemed completely unconcerned about driving a rust-bucket through the grounds of the Blumen Estate. She couldn't quite bring herself to say anything. Jessa knew money was tight and a new car just wasn't in the budget.

"How come you've never been here before?" her mother asked.

Jessa shrugged and picked at the shiny bow. It must have seemed strange to her mother that Rachel wasn't one of Jessa's best friends. Jessa's mother knew better than anyone her daughter's passion for anything to do with horses.

The truth was, Jessa thought Rachel was a bit of a snob. She had been more than a little surprised when both she and her best friend, Cheryl Waters, had received invitations.

She was saved from having to come up with an explanation when her mother suddenly hit the brakes at a fork in the driveway.

"Whoops! I nearly overshot the turnoff."

A huge bunch of balloons and streamers hung from a tree branch and bobbed gently in the breeze. A carved sign at the fork to the right read, "Stables."

Jessa guessed the main drive continued up to the house.

The car backed up and then made the turn towards the barn. Jessa unlocked her door and waited with her hand on the door handle as they pulled into a wide, circular driveway in front of the stables. She wanted to escape from the clunker and her mother's questions as quickly as possible.

Jessa jumped out of the car as it pulled to a stop and gave her mother a quick wave. She wasn't fast enough, though. Krista and Bridget, two friends who also attended Grade Six at Kenwood Elementary, ran from the barn to meet her.

"Hi Jessa!"

"Come on—Rachel's up in the hayloft with every-one else. We're just waiting for you!"

Jessa turned to follow the girls into the barn. She cringed as her mother honked the horn and waved good-bye. Jessa ran after her friends and ignored her mother. She hoped nobody else noticed when the car backfired again as it pulled away from the barn.

Jessa paused just inside the stable door and blinked. Her eyes took a moment to adjust to the dim light of the barn after the brilliant sunshine of the yard.

Two rows of box stalls stretched along either side of a wide alleyway. The barn was quiet and spotless.

"Come on, Jessa!"

Bridget appeared from inside a box stall.

"Where are the horses?" Jessa asked.

"They've all been turned out. Hurry up!"

Bridget disappeared back into the empty stall and

Jessa slowly followed her. A thick layer of golden straw was spread on the ground. Bridget was nowhere in sight.

"Up here!"

Jessa looked up and saw three faces peering down at her through a trap door. Bridget, Krista and Rachel were all grinning down through the hay chute above the manger.

"Come on, climb up. . . . "

"Pass the present up here. . . ."

Jessa stared at the manger in front of her. *What if she fell?* She felt her neck begin to turn red. She tried to balance the present in one hand and pull herself forward and up onto the manger. Her foot was in an awkward position and she couldn't see a good place to hold on. The girls shouted encouragement and suggestions but the more helpful they tried to be, the more tense she felt. She wished they would just be quiet.

"Pass the present up!"

"Here—give me your hand."

"Put your other foot up higher."

Jessa wobbled precariously for a moment. Her left foot teetered on the edge of the manger. She reached her hand up and felt Rachel's fingers brush her own. And then, as if everything was moving at half normal speed, Jessa began to fall. She pushed away from the wall and half-jumped and half-staggered backwards into the hay. She landed ungraciously on her rump.

"Ouch!"

"Are you okay?" Krista called.

The three girls scrambled down through the hole of the hay chute and one by one hopped off the manger and gathered around Jessa.

Jessa picked up the present from where it had fallen in the straw. She brushed it off and hastily stood up, pushing her glasses back into position.

"Maybe you should take the stairs," suggested Krista. Jessa's stomach clenched.

"Yeah, I guess maybe I should," she mumbled.

What a great start to a party. She just wanted to go home.

Jessa followed the other girls through the tack room. Rows of saddles lined both walls. Bridles hung neatly from hooks. Above each hook was the name of a horse . . . Jasper, Moonstone, Eliza Jane, Gazelle, Ruby. . . .

Jessa felt an unhappy squeeze in the pit of her stomach. *It just wasn't fair. She would never have a horse, never!*

As the other girls reached the door at the back of the tack room, Jessa heard Rachel whisper to Krista, "my mom made me invite her and Cheryl."

"Good thing your uncle's a lawyer," Krista whispered back, just loudly enough for Jessa to hear. "*Someone* might fall off while they're riding and sue you."

Rachel nudged Krista in the ribs and they disappeared through the door. The sound of their boots pounding up the stairs filled Jessa's head.

Alone in the tack room, Jessa felt like throwing her present on the floor and stepping on it. Angrily, she took her glasses off and wiped her eyes. She wasn't going to give Rachel the satisfaction of seeing her cry.

She heard footsteps coming down the stairs from the hayloft and quickly put her glasses back on.

Now what? Why couldn't Rachel just leave her alone?

"Hey, Jessa. Rachel said you were here. Are you staying down here all day?"

"Cheryl!" Jessa smiled at her best friend with relief. Cheryl walked around behind her.

"Wow! Great hair! I wish mine was long enough for a French braid."

Jessa grinned. She couldn't imagine Cheryl with anything other than her short, red hair. Cheryl wasn't the French braid type.

"My mom did it this morning," Jessa said. Then she sighed. "I don't want to go up there," she added.

Cheryl pushed her eyebrows together and drew herself up tall. She put on a prim, old fashioned, school-teacherly voice.

"Not getting along with Miss Rachel? Why ever not?"

Jessa shrugged. "How did you know?"

Cheryl didn't answer right away. She closed her eyes and drew in a long, hissing breath through pursed lips. Slowly she lifted her arms and then, with great concentration, pressed her fingertips to her temples.

"Intuition," she whispered dramatically.

Cheryl's dream was to be an actor like her parents.

They ran a small theatre company and sometimes Cheryl did small parts in their plays. Jessa was used to her friend's sometimes outrageous accents and crazy antics.

Half the time, Jessa was embarrassed to death to be seen in public with her best friend.

Now, though, she was glad to be distracted by Cheryl's impression of a psychic.

"I predict we are missing the paaaaarty," Cheryl moaned. "I see a hayloft . . . wait, wait . . . and rectangular blocks of . . . ah, yes! Hay bales!"

"Let us go then, you and I . . ." she said, switching voices to one of mock romance.

Cheryl's other annoying habit was quoting poetry. The opening stanza of *The Love Song of J. Alfred Prufrock* was one of her favourite selections.

". . . when the evening is laid out against the sky . . ." Jessa added. She had heard the poem so often she, too, knew it by heart.

". . . like a patient etherized upon the table," the girls finished in unison.

They made their way together up the narrow staircase which led to the hayloft.

Jessa ignored Rachel and sat beside Cheryl on an empty hay bale.

"Let's do the presents now!" suggested Krista.

"No, I want to ride!" said Monika, a plump girl wearing jodhpurs and a white shirt.

"Are you still taking lessons with Patty McBride?" asked Sarah who sat beside Monika. "I haven't seen you on Wednesdays for a while."

Everyone who even dreamed of owning a horse and taking lessons knew who Patty McBride was. She was the best coach on the West Coast and both Sarah and Monika took lessons from her every week.

"I just changed days so I could go out on a trail first," explained Monika.

Jessa picked a piece of straw out of Cheryl's hair. *What could she contribute to this conversation?* Not much. Her mother flat out refused to buy her a horse. Even her weekly riding lesson on a school horse at Arbutus Lane Equestrian Centre stretched the family budget to the limit—and that wasn't with Patty McBride.

Monika owned a horse and Sarah had a full lease on a bay thoroughbred. Both girls kept their horses at Arbutus Lane. Of course, Rachel Blumen had the best horse of all—a purebred Arabian mare called Gazelle—nearly pure white and able to jump just about anything.

Jessa sighed and looked down at her inexpensive rubber riding boots. The other girls were either wearing high leather boots or fancy paddock boots. She half hoped they wouldn't ride after all so nobody would notice her ugly footwear. She couldn't imagine what the others would think if they knew she had bought them second-hand at a used tack sale.

Rachel checked her watch. "We can ride in about an hour," she said, staring straight at Jessa. "That's when Jeremy and Rebecca will be here. My mom asked them to come to help *some* of you with tacking up."

"Who is Jeremy?" asked Jessa defensively, trying not to get too annoyed about Rachel's pointed comment.

Rachel and Monika gasped in mock horror.

"You mean you don't know Jeremy?" giggled Rachel.

Jessa noticed Krista and Bridget were being very quiet. She looked to the others for help.

"Yeah, Jessa. Don't you know who Jeremy is?" asked Bridget.

Jessa suspected Bridget had no idea, either.

Bridget nudged Krista beside her on the bale of hay.

"Yeah, Jessa. Where have you been recently?" asked Krista quickly, joining in the teasing.

Jessa blushed again. She had no idea whom they were talking about. But she was hardly going to admit it!

Cheryl piped up loudly, "So . . . do tell. Who is this Jeremy person?" Her strong voice filled the hay loft.

Cheryl winked at Jessa. "Fear not, my dear. We shall soon get to the bottom of this."

"Jeremy just happens to be the cutest boy around," gushed Rachel.

"He rides a gorgeous black Andalusian," added Monika.

"He is soooo . . . sooooo . . ." Sarah was at a complete loss for words. "Well, I'm going to pretend I've never tacked up before, so he'll help me," she said finally.

Sarah rubbed the toe of her polished riding boot with the inside of her cuff. She was very tall and slim and always managed to look elegant, even in gym class.

"Jeremy boards his horse, Caspian, here," explained Rachel. "That's why I know him so well. I have to admit it was one of my mother's better ideas to have him help with the party."

Several of the girls giggled. Jessa looked at her boots. She didn't find the conversation funny at all.

"Rebecca is his mother. She's one of the best trainers in Western Canada. She works with my dad sometimes," said Rachel smugly.

"His mother?" groaned Cheryl dramatically. "Oh great. No smoochie smoochie in the box stalls for Rachel!"

Cheryl made loud kissing noises and rolled her eyes. The girls laughed hysterically and Monika slipped off the end of her hay bale.

How did Cheryl do it? Nobody ever laughed at anything Jessa said.

The girls were giggling so loudly, none of the them heard Rachel's father calling from the tack room.

"Girls!" he shouted.

Rachel glared at her friends. "Shhhhh. . . ." They all stifled their laughter and listened as Mr. Blumen came up the stairs.

"You mother is waiting for you in the house.

11

Bring your friends in so they can have something to eat and play a few games before you ride."

"But . . ." started Rachel.

Her father put up his hand to silence her.

"Rachel, come right now. No argument! I won't have any more of this."

He turned and left. The girls sat quietly, not knowing quite what to do next. Rachel stared at the ground. Jessa and Cheryl exchanged awkward glances. *What a grouch to have for a father!*

"What was that all about?" asked Cheryl.

"Oh, nothing," grumbled Rachel.

"Should we go up to the house?" asked Krista, looking nervously at the head of the stairs as if she expected Rachel's father to reappear at any moment.

"I guess so," said Rachel. And then, with anger and frustration in her voice she added, "I *told* them we were too old for stupid party games but they wouldn't listen."

Jessa scuffed her boots in the loose hay on the ground. "It's okay," she said. "My mom's like that, too. I don't mind—we can play games until it's time to ride."

"Yeah, no problem," added Krista.

"Lucky your dad lives in Japan," whispered Cheryl.

"My dad's not like that!" Jessa whispered back.

"Come on, girls—let's party!" said Cheryl, leaping off the end of her hay bale.

The girls filed out of the hay loft. Jessa couldn't

quite decipher the look on Rachel's face when she brushed past her. It was part relief, part embarrassment and part anger. Jessa fell into step beside Cheryl and together they headed up to the rambling ranch house on the hill.

Chapter Two

"So?"

"So what?" answered Jessa, poking her spoon around her wheat flakes.

"The party? How was the birthday party?"

"It was okay, I guess."

"That doesn't sound too enthusiastic. I thought you were the girl who loved horses?"

Jessa shrugged. There was no way her mother would understand why she had been so miserable at Rachel's birthday party. It sounded stupid to say that she was the only one with rubber boots, the only one who didn't own a riding helmet, the only one who had to ride in jeans. Even Cheryl owned an old pair of jods she'd inherited from her older cousin. Cheryl wasn't even a serious rider!

And how could she explain the humiliation of being given old Roger to ride? Roger, the retired farm mascot who spent most of his days grazing out in the sunny fields of the Blumen Estate, was the only horse Rachel said would be 'safe' enough for Jessa.

In fact, by the time the riding part of the party

arrived, Jessa had decided Rachel deserved to have a bad-tempered father.

"Jessa Marie Richardson. . . ."

Jessa sighed. When her mom said her name in that slow, serious way there was no way to get out of having "A TALK."

"I think it's time we had a talk. Tell me what's wrong. You've been drooping around like a sick pigeon ever since you got home yesterday."

"A sick pigeon? Mom, please. There's nothing you can do about it. Just forget about it, okay?"

Jessa stared into her bowl of cereal and hoped desperately her mother would just go away. Dumb Rachel. Even after Jessa had pointed out she had started jumping in her riding lessons, Rachel had been adamant that Cheryl and Jessa take turns on Roger.

The poor old thing practically creaked when he walked. She and Cheryl had felt sorry for him so they had spent most of the time letting him graze while they talked in the shade of a big oak tree.

"I don't blame you two for not riding much," Rachel had said as she and the other girls had headed off to the riding ring. "He can be a bit hard to handle."

"Jessa, are you listening to me?" Jessa looked up at her mother. "I don't want to play twenty guesses. Does this have something to do with wanting a horse of your own?"

Jessa shrugged again. She bit the inside of her cheek and forced herself not to cry when she spoke.

"It's okay, Mom. I know we can't afford it. We need a car and the deck is falling apart and we have to save up to get a new washing machine and until you finish school and start working full-time. . . ."

Jessa couldn't stop herself. She burst into tears as she thought of all the things they needed before she was ever likely to get a horse. She felt her mother's hands on her shoulders.

"Oh, Jessa. Maybe you could find out about a few extra lessons or something."

Jessa pulled in her breath in short, sharp jerks. Lessons were so frustrating! They were expensive and she still couldn't really do what she wanted on a school horse. And even worse, they only lasted one short hour each week. It always seemed she had hardly mounted up before it was time to get off again.

"Okay," she whispered softly. Her mother was trying to do the best she could. She just didn't understand how hard it was to be patient.

"Jessa, if we can just hang in long enough for me to get my accounting designation we'll be laughing. You can have your horse *and* I can buy a decent car."

Jessa nodded and wiped her eyes with the back of her hand. She wished she could tell her mother that it didn't really matter, that a horse was a luxury she could live quite well without. All she could manage was a teary nod. Sure, maybe one day her mother would finish school and get a great job and Jessa would get her horse. Yeah, sure, it *could* happen—and maybe one day pigs would fly.

The next afternoon Jessa finished her homework quickly and flopped down on her bed to read. Her room was small and cozy, tucked up under the eaves of the little old house where she lived with her mom. Jessa loved her room and the view out the window. When she was lying on her bed she could see the tangle of branches of an old apple tree.

Jessa liked to imagine she lived in the country in an old farmhouse and that if she walked out the kitchen door she would find herself in a country garden with cooking herbs growing right by the door and a little path which led out to the chicken coop and the barn.

When she sat up, the view changed—the roof tops of the other houses in her neighborhood appeared and her imaginary farm life faded away.

Jessa's room clearly belonged to someone who was completely horse crazy. There was a huge poster of a mare and foal on the back of her door, pictures and posters of horses covered every inch of available wall space, and her shelves were filled with horse books and models. Nailed to the headboard of her bed were 16 horseshoes, all with open ends pointing up so her luck wouldn't run out.

She had a special lightweight aluminum shoe from a trip to the racetrack, and a giant draft horse shoe which she got from a working farm holiday she'd been on two years earlier. She had a shoe from the first school pony she had ever ridden and others collected from farriers who happened to be at the barn at the same time as Jessa. Somehow, of all the horsey things she owned, she liked the shoes best.

Jessa figured she had more horseshoes than most horse owners bothered to keep.

Jessa sat up on her bed and looked over at her reflection in the dresser mirror. What did a 'real' rider look like? Not like the plain girl with glasses, mousy shoulder-length hair and a definite slouch who looked back at her..

She drew herself up as tall as she could and held an imaginary pair of reins in her hands. She clucked encouragement and urged her mount on. She turned her hazel eyes forward and lifted her chin.

"Ladies and Gentlemen . . . Entering the ring now is Miss Jessa Richardson on her mount Starfire."

"Jessa?"

Jessa heard a quiet tap at her bedroom door. She hastily dropped her imaginary reins and flopped back down on the bed, fumbling for her book.

"Yes?"

Jessa's mom came in and sat on the bed beside her. Jessa glanced down at her novel and realized with a start she was holding it upside-down! She blushed and quickly put it down. To Jessa's relief, her mother hadn't even noticed.

"I've been thinking about this horse problem," she said.

"You have?"

Jessa's mother looked at her reproachfully. "Well, my dear girl, your mile-long face is hard to miss."

Jessa grinned cheekily. "So, what have you been thinking, Mommy darling?" She put her arm around her mother's slender shoulders.

"Do you remember Brenda from my tax law class?"

"Ummm . . . no. Should I?"

"It doesn't matter. Her daughter used to ride before she discovered boys."

Jessa's mother paused and looked directly at her daughter.

"Hey! Don't worry! I have no intention of discovering boys—ever! I swear!"

"Hmmm . . . " her mother groaned. "Anyway, I had lunch with Brenda yesterday and she said the tack store has a bulletin board where people sometimes post notices about horses for lease."

True, thought Jessa. *But what about the money? It was still expensive to lease a horse and then on top of that pay for feed and shoes and lessons and. . . .*

"Now, you know we can't afford a horse at the moment," her mother continued, as if reading Jessa's mind. "But Brenda was telling me how, when her car needed brakes, she traded the garage book-keeping services for work on her car."

Jessa had no idea where her mother was going with her story about Brenda's broken brakes.

"So, I thought maybe I could offer to trade my services as an almost-accountant for at least part of what it would cost to lease a horse for you. Since the biggest part of the monthly expenses seems to be board—maybe I could work something out with a stable like Arbutus Lane. They have a big operation, I'm sure they could use some help doing their books."

Jessa's heart fell. Somehow, her mother's plan sounded a bit far-fetched. Even so, when she suggested they make a trip to the tack store to check the notice board, Jessa quickly got ready. As far as she was concerned, the tack store was the best shop in town. Even the smell of the place was great.

That evening, Jessa's mother began making phone calls. After the third person had turned her mother's offer down, Jessa retreated to her room and sat at her desk.

She stared at her poster of mares and foals grazing in a mountain valley. The contours of the horses' backs matched the rolling folds of the mountains behind them. Jessa often wondered if the photographer had posed the horses that way; the scene seemed too perfect to be real.

She fished a pen out of her pencil case and began to write a letter.

Dear Dad,
Hi. How are you? I am fine.
Could you please send me enough
money for a horse?

Jessa crumpled up the letter and tossed it towards her waste basket. The ball bounced off the rim and rolled under her bed.

She could hardly remember her father. She hadn't seen him since he left when she was two years old. There was no point in asking him for money, she knew that. He was a technician who worked at a radio station in Tokyo.

He had a new wife and a baby and when he occasionally did write, he always said something about how expensive everything was in Japan.

Mostly, he tried to forget he had ever lived in Canada. Last year, he had even managed to forget Jessa's birthday.

There was a tap at Jessa's door.

"Come in!"

Her mother came in and sat on the bed.

"Hmmmm . . . " she started thoughtfully. "So far, no luck. But I left a couple of messages on answering machines, so you never know." She smiled at her daughter. "Cheer up, Pumpkin. We'll figure something out. I'm going to make a little poster on the computer and put it up at the tack store. Maybe that will catch someone's eye."

"Yeah, maybe," Jessa mumbled.

"Hi, Jessa!"

Jessa hurried along the aisle at the Equestrian Centre. She was nearly late for her lesson. She waved at Jimmy McBride, the barn manager and Patty McBride's husband.

"You're riding King today. He's already in the cross-ties."

"Thanks, Jimmy!"

Good. At least King usually picked up the correct lead.

Jessa sighed. It was so hard being on a different horse each week. She picked up a grooming caddy from the tack room and walked up to King.

You may as well get used to this, Jessa, she thought to herself. Things weren't likely to change any time soon.

"Well, what do you think?" Jessa's mother asked.

Jessa eyed the neon pink piece of paper her mother held up as they sat down for dinner.

"Fish cakes? Again? Do we have any ketchup?"

"Jessa! I'm doing this for you. Do you have any better ideas?"

Jessa sighed and dutifully studied the sign more carefully.

HORSE LEASE WANTED
In exchange for book-keeping services.

"Whatever. It's worth a try, I guess," she said finally. "Do we have any ketchup, or not?"

"It's in the fridge where it always is. Why don't you get some for both of us?"

Mother and daughter ate dinner in stony silence. The longer she sat there saying nothing, the worse Jessa felt.

She wanted to say that lessons were fine, that she didn't need her own horse, but the words were stuck somewhere deep inside, down in the dark place she kept all her lies.

Jessa pushed her food around with her fork. At the best of times she didn't like fish cakes.

"Why don't you just go to your room?"

There was no anger in her mother's voice. Just weariness.

Without argument, Jessa went upstairs and quietly closed her bedroom door.

When Jessa came home from school the next day she headed straight for the closet under the stairs. She pulled out the vacuum cleaner and got to work—first the living room, then the hallway and finally, the stairs.

She worked quickly, hurrying to get finished before her mother arrived home from the college.

When the vacuum cleaner was back in its place, she cleared the breakfast dishes away and put on the kettle. By the time her mother walked in, a fresh pot of tea was on the table.

"Thank you! What a nice surprise!" she said, dropping a huge pile of books on the couch. "Tea! Just what I need."

Jessa pulled a note from her pocket and offered it to her mother.

"What's this?"

"Just read it," Jessa mumbled.

Jessa's mother read the apology silently and then gave her daughter a quick hug. "Thank you, Jessa."

At lunch the next day, Cheryl and Jessa continued their daily contest to see who could jump farther off their swings.

"Hey! Is that your mom?" Cheryl asked. Jessa stopped pumping her swing and peered towards the fence by the edge of the school yard. A woman with short, dark hair and a bright red coat was waving her arms at the two girls.

"It sure looks like her! What's she doing here?"

Jessa and Cheryl leaped from their swings and raced to the fence.

"Jessa!" her mother said as they arrived in a whirl of flying arms and legs. "Guess what!"

"I was talking to Brenda after class and she said her daughter knows of someone who has a pony for lease." Her mother looked at Jessa as if waiting for an answer.

"For lease?" Jessa asked, not knowing quite where the conversation was going.

"A free lease, actually."

"What's a free lease?" Cheryl asked.

Jessa's heart thumped—she could hardly believe what she was hearing.

"Have you ever heard of a free lease before?" Jessa's mother asked.

Jessa nodded enthusiastically.

"What's a free lease?" Cheryl asked again.

"I thought it was more for old horses the owners don't *really* want to get rid of," said Jessa.

"Oh," her mother said. "I didn't think to ask how *old* this pony is."

"What pony?" Jessa asked.

"Would somebody please tell me what a free lease is?" Cheryl insisted.

"Shhh. What pony, Mom?"

"I don't know too much about him. Remember tax law Brenda?"

Jessa nodded.

"Her daughter used to ride with the girl who used to lease him. Rebel, I think that's his name."

"Rebel?"

"I suppose that other girl also had a mysterious *free lease?*" Cheryl asked.

"Shhh." Jessa poked her friend in the ribs.

"I don't know. But the girl bought her own horse several months ago. So, now nobody is riding the pony."

"Not even on a free lease basis," Cheryl said.

Jessa elbowed her harder. "Be quiet!"

"So, here's the story. Brenda phoned the owner, a lady called Rosa, and told her all about you. Apparently, Rosa has several other horses and doesn't really have room for Rebel. As I understand it, we would have to pay for all the pony's expenses—board, shoes, worming, all that horse stuff you know more about than I do."

"So, what's free about all this?" Cheryl asked.

Jessa's mother ignored her and went on. "In return, you would be the only one riding Rebel. I guess she would take him back if you weren't looking after him properly. I know it's not quite the same as owning. . . ."

"What . . . is. . . ."

"Cheryl! Be quiet!" Jessa hissed. "The bell's going to ring in a minute!"

25

"I'm going to pick you up after school so we can go and have a look at him. Rosa wants to meet you."

The bell rang to signal the end of the lunch hour.

"Oh no!" Jessa groaned.

How could she possibly concentrate all afternoon?

"Come straight out! Don't forget!" her mother called after the girls as they joined the others going into the red brick building.

"Jessa?" Cheryl asked.

"What?"

"How are you guys going to afford all that food and stuff? And where are you going to keep him? And what if he's really old or ugly or lame or something?"

Jessa was almost glad when they reached their desks so she didn't have to talk to Cheryl any more. Even if the pony turned out to be okay she had no idea how they would manage this 'free' lease.

She crossed her fingers under her desk and thought hard of all her lucky horseshoes. She would need the luck of all sixteen of them to find a barn whose owner needed a good bookkeeper in exchange for boarding a pony called Rebel.

Chapter Three

Jessa ran full tilt down the front steps of the school and tore open the car door. She threw her books on the back seat and buckled up.

"I called the owner of the horse. Rosa and I had a nice, long chat," her mother said.

Jessa's mother passed her a list.

Horse Expenses
-board
-feed
-shoes
-worming
-vet
-shots
-tack
-grooming supplies
-shipping bandages
-lessons
-show expenses
-trailering
-vitamins
-horse blankets
-fly hood

"I don't think this is complete. I think we might have a problem here."

Jessa stared at the list. Her mother had been doing her homework. Jessa stared blankly at her mother's neat handwriting. Like every list she wrote, everything was perfectly lined up and under the last item she had a double underline.

Each item on the list represented money, more money than her mother had.

"Maybe we shouldn't go and look," Jessa said slowly. "I mean, if we can't. . . ."

"Shhh. We will figure out a way to do this. I made a few phone calls this afternoon."

"What kind of calls?"

"About trading book-keeping for board. I talked to that nice man at Arbutus Lane."

"Jimmy? What did he say?

"They already have an accountant."

"Oh."

"He suggested a couple of the other barns in the area I could try. He didn't think it was a strange idea at all."

"What did the other barns say?"

"I couldn't get hold of anyone so I left messages. Hopefully, we'll hear back soon."

"What if everyone says 'no'?"

Jessa's mother thoughtfully chewed on her bottom lip.

"Can you remember when I really wanted my own office at home?"

Jessa remembered very well. After the divorce, she

and her mother had moved into the little house on Desdemona Street. Her mother had taken the tiny bedroom which was barely big enough for her double bed.

Jessa and all her toys had moved into the roomy master bedroom. When her mother had wanted to study, she had to spread her books out on the dining room table.

"It was awful," her mom said. "I had no room for anything. Everything I needed for my work was piled up all over the place. We had even less money than we do now and all I could think of was how great it would be to have a bit more room of my own, a real office to work in with a big desk and space for my books. I could never find anything! It was terrible."

"What does this have to do with the horse?" asked Jessa.

"Well, at the time it seemed impossible to do renovations on the house. And then, one day you were in the garden on your apple tree swing. Do you remember?"

Jessa nodded. She remembered how, when she was at the highest point of her arc, she could just see a tiny window tucked up under the eaves of their little house.

"Where does that window go, Mommy," she had asked.

"When you asked me that, a little light went on in my head. That's when I thought of fixing up the attic for you and using my bedroom for an office."

"I'm glad you had that thought," Jessa smiled. She loved her cozy room at the top of the steep, narrow stairs.

"I had never held a hammer before I started fixing up that room for you."

"Mom, you're not thinking of building a barn in the back yard, are you?"

"No, you silly goose," her mother laughed. "But I do believe that if you imagine hard enough what you'd really like more than anything, that somehow, you'll find a way to get it."

Jessa closed her eyes and imagined herself leading a lovely horse into a comfortable box stall. She rested her head back against the seat and let the hum of the car drown out her doubts. *Even if it wasn't very realistic*, Jessa thought, *it certainly was a pleasant picture.*

As they drove out into the green, rolling farmland of the Saanich Peninsula, Jessa's mother filled her in on the few details she had managed to find out over the phone.

"He isn't huge, just 14 hands, but Rosa says he's kind."

When Jessa had heard all about him once, she insisted her mother repeat every detail again.

Rebel was a bay, Welsh-Quarter horse cross— stocky and strong. He hadn't been ridden much for quite a while. Rosa thought he might be a bit fresh.

A bit fresh? Jessa wondered how wild the little pony would be. *Would she be able to ride him? Would he buck her off? Would Rosa think she could handle him?* Jessa wiped over her riding boots nervously. She

30

was wearing her jeans. She really had to get a pair of jodhpurs—and she didn't have a proper riding shirt. She wished she could magically transform her rubber riding boots into a beautiful pair of fine leather boots from Italy. She wondered if the barn was a fancy hunter barn where the correct outfit was almost as important as how well one rode.

As they drove farther and farther out into the country, down one small road and then another, Jessa wondered how anyone ever found the riding stable. Eventually, as they drove down a muddy, potholed driveway behind a ramshackle old trailer home, Jessa realized the "barn" was just a three-sided shed.

Several tired-looking horses were standing knee-deep in mud, picking at some hay which was spread in the muck. They hardly looked up as Jessa and her mother stepped out of the car.

A wiry little woman came out of the trailer and waved.

"Hello there! I'm Rosa. You must be Jessa. You're a bit early—I'll grab a halter."

Jessa stared at the horses in the muddy paddock. She couldn't see a pony in the lot. She looked around for another paddock or a proper barn.

"Rebel!" shouted Rosa as she banged out of a little metal tool shed with a frayed halter in her hand.

"Rebel!"

First a black nose and then a pair of inquisitive ears poked out from behind the shelter. Jessa could see they belonged to a pony who had been hidden from view.

"Come on, baby!"

As the pony stepped into view, Jessa's heart dropped into her boots. This was not the horse she had dreamed of.

The pony was a mess. He was covered from head to tail in thick sticky mud. His long, black mane and tail were matted and full of bits of hay and twigs. Somewhere under all the mud there was, she supposed, a dark brown horse, but he could have been a palomino for all she could see of him.

Rosa let herself into the paddock and picked her way through the puddles. Rebel didn't look too fresh at all when she slipped the halter over his ears and led him back towards the gate.

Rosa tied him to the fence and retrieved a bucket of brushes from the shed. She threw an old saddle onto the top rail of the fence and winked at Jessa as if she were sharing a big secret.

"There you go—groom him, tack him up and have a little ride. He's a sweetheart, he is."

Rosa gave the filthy pony a slap on the rump and winked again as a cloud of dust rose up above him.

"Have fun. Call me when you're through and we'll have a little talk. I'll be in the house."

Jessa ran her hand over the pony's shoulder. It came away black with dirt.

"Oh, Jessa. I'm so sorry. It's okay if you don't want to ride him. He's so . . . so . . . scruffy," her mother said finally.

But Jessa didn't answer. The pony was looking at her thoughtfully, his large, dark eyes soft and curious. He reached towards her slowly and gently lipped her jacket sleeve.

"Is he biting you?" her mother asked nervously.

Jessa laughed and held her hand out, palm open, to Rebel. He sniffed her hand and then gently licked it. He nodded his head as if to say he approved of the taste and then started to lick more vigorously.

No, this wasn't a nippy pony. He was probably bored out of his head having to stand around in a muddy paddock all day.

"It's okay, Mom. I'll take him on a little ride down the road and back."

"Are you sure?"

Jessa wiped her wet hand on her jeans and then picked up a curry comb. She began to work on his neck. She hadn't reached his withers before she was so warm she had to stop and take off her coat.

Even though it took ages to get Rebel reasonably clean, he stood patiently and quietly as she worked. He picked up his feet quickly and only puffed himself up slightly when Jessa tightened his girth. She put on the bridle and led him in a small circle. Jessa felt the little horse at her side, waiting to see what she would do next.

"You know, Mom. . . ."

"I know, Jessa. You are falling in love," her mother answered before she could finish her thought.

As Jessa mounted Rebel she blushed and smiled.

"I guess I am," she said, and turned the pony to ride out the long driveway.

By the time Jessa got back from her ride there was no doubt in her mind that Rebel was the horse for her. She talked non-stop as she untacked him and brushed him once again.

"I can clean him up—that's no problem—and I'll get some shoes on the front—he was a little tender when we went on the gravel—I can ask Rachel or Monika about who the best farrier is around here. His hay belly doesn't matter, either—I'll just start him out slow and then build up as he gets fitter."

"Jessa?" her mother interrupted the steady stream of horse-talk. "We have to talk about where to keep him."

Jessa was quiet for a minute. "I know that sometimes Arbutus Lane Equestrian Centre will trade work, you know, doing stalls and stuff, for board. I could talk to Jimmy. He may not need an accountant, but I know he has lots of stalls to clean! Could we stop there on the way home?"

Her mother gave her a quick hug. "That's my girl," she said. "We'll figure something out. I'll go and find Rosa and let her know you'd like to give him a try."

Jessa didn't tell her mother the rest of the story, how Arbutus Lane was usually overrun with girls wanting to trade for lessons, or board—how hard it might be to actually get a job there, especially as she had no stable management experience. Jessa swallowed hard and ran her hand along Rebel's scruffy neck. *What would she do if she couldn't find a place to keep him?*

As she turned him back out into the wet paddock she thought she would start to cry. *If she couldn't convince Jimmy to let her work off her board, what would she do?* Rebel looked back over his shoulder at her.

"I'll be back, Rebel," she whispered. "Don't worry."

But inside, Jessa didn't feel nearly so confident.

The parking lot at Arbutus Lane was crowded with cars. The big hunter-jumper establishment was always busy.

Jessa walked into the main barn. To her left, a long row of box stalls stretched along a spotless aisle. To her right was the indoor riding ring. There was another aisle with roomy box stalls on the far side of the ring. At the end of the building was a glassed-in viewing lounge overlooking the riding ring. A small group of spectators watched horses and riders practicing over several colourful jumps.

As Jessa passed each stall she wondered about the horses who lived there. Some of them eagerly poked their heads out of their stalls at the sound of her approaching footsteps. Others hung back and ignored her completely. Some stalls were empty—their occupants either outside in their walk-out paddocks, or being ridden.

Each stall door had a nameplate with the horse's name carved into a piece of dark wood and painted in gold lettering.

Jessa set her chin and decided to put her mother's theory about imagining her own perfect world into existence.

REBEL of ARBUTUS LANE.'

Jessa imagined Rebel's friendly ears perked forward as she arrived to take him out for a ride along one of the many trails which criss-crossed the 120 acres of the large horse facility. She pictured herself leading him down the aisle to the grooming area before mounting up for a lesson in the large indoor ring. She could hardly wait until she and Rebel moved in.

As Jessa neared the door to the stable office, she became more and more nervous. By the time she raised her hand to knock, her mouth was dry and her palms were sweaty. Her heart hammered in her chest and she felt as if it might explode.

"Come in," Jimmy called abruptly.

Jessa walked into the small office. There were photos everywhere of horses with winning ribbons fastened to their bridles and smiling riders holding trophies. Jimmy was on the phone and gestured for Jessa to sit down. As she waited for him to finish his conversation, she studied the rows and rows of ribbons and trophies displayed behind his desk.

"Fine. Drop it by on Friday—I'll make sure to have a couple of bodies on hand to help you unload."

He hung up the phone and ran his hand through his dark, thinning hair.

"Hay!" he said with a snort. "Never had so much

trouble finding decent hay in my life!"

Jessa nodded. She wasn't quite sure if she would recognize good hay or not. It all looked like dried grass to her.

"Hi, Jessa," he said. "You want to sign up for more lessons?"

"No . . . I mean . . . yes . . . I mean—well, yes, but that's not why I'm here," Jessa blurted out.

Jimmy raised his eyebrows and leaned back in his chair with his arms folded across his chest.

Jessa bumbled on, tripping over her words.

"I was just wondering if, well, if you maybe could use some help . . . you know, around here in the barn. . . . You see, I'm just getting this new horse and I can't really afford a lot for board and . . . I just thought . . . well. . . ."

Jimmy looked at Jessa seriously, his dark eyebrows pushed together. Jessa squirmed under his steady gaze.

"Do you know how much it costs to board a horse here?" he asked finally.

Jessa shook her head. "No—not exactly," she admitted.

Jimmy told her. Jessa closed her eyes and bit her lower lip. The amount was even more than she had guessed.

"That's a lot of hours of work," he continued. "And you do still have the inconvenience of going to school every day?"

Jessa nodded. She wished she could just disappear. *What had she been thinking to come in here and ask about a job?*

37

Jessa looked back at him over his desk littered with piles of papers, horse magazines and several well-chewed pens.

"I'm a fast learner and a hard worker," she said finally, but without a trace of hope in her voice.

"Jessa," he said, not unkindly. "I like you. You're a good student, you do work hard in your lessons. But the older girls who have been here for years already have the after school and weekend work. I can add you to the list but I'll be honest with you, there are a lot of good kids ahead of you already."

"Where do you keep your horse now?" he asked.

Jessa sighed. She thought she was going to cry. "I don't keep him anywhere . . . and if I don't find somewhere, then I might not even be able to get him at all . . . I . . . Ohhhh . . ." Jessa sobbed and looked down at the floor. "I'm sorry I bothered you . . . I'll just go . . ." she said and stood up.

"Sit down," ordered Jimmy, not unkindly. "Here." He handed her a red and white bandanna which she took gratefully and wiped her eyes.

"I'm sorry, but I just can't do anything right at the moment." He shook his head. "It might help if you could get some experience at a smaller barn."

Jimmy stopped mid-sentence. "You know, I just thought of something."

A slow smile spread over his ruddy face and his cheeks flushed. "When I first moved to Victoria, I was only thirteen. I knew I wanted to compete. My dream, even then, was to be an eventer. But I had no idea how to find a decent horse."

Jimmy stood up and reached for a framed photograph standing on the shelf behind his desk. He handed the photo to Jessa. She looked closely at the boy of about fourteen proudly holding a large trophy in both hands. He stood beside a chestnut horse. A woman with brown hair and a wide smile stood at the horse's head.

"Is this you?" she asked.

"Jimmy nodded. "And that's the horse who really got my career started. Chocolate BonBon was his name—but we called him Bonny Boy."

"Is that lady your mother?"

Jimmy laughed. "No, no. My mother is afraid of horses. No. That's Mrs. Bailey. She owned the horse. And, for whatever reason, she decided to take a chance on a kid she hardly knew. Maybe she'll do it again."

"What do you mean?" Jessa asked.

Jimmy didn't explain. "Do you have time to let me make a quick phone call?"

Jimmy didn't give her a chance to respond. He picked up the phone and dialled.

"B. B.—It's Jimmy! How are you? Good. Fine, fine. Busy, as always. Listen, I'm actually calling on behalf of a young friend of mine. Are you still looking for someone to help you out over at your barn? Yes? Wonderful, wonderful. Yes, I have a young woman here who happens to be looking for a place for her horse—she needs to work off her board—Should I send her over? Fine, I'll do that." He chatted for a few more minutes and then hung up the phone.

Jessa held her breath and waited for Jimmy to speak after he hung up.

"It's not quite like this place, but if Mrs. Bailey takes a liking to you, you and your horse will do fine over at Dark Creek Stables. Here's the address. If you head over there now, Mrs. Bailey will meet you at the end of her driveway."

"Oh thank you, thank you so much," Jessa said as she got up to leave.

"Jessa?"

"Yes?"

"You'll never work harder in your life. But she can teach you an awful lot."

Chapter Four

Jessa's head was spinning as she ran back to the car. She repeated the instructions to her mother and they drove down the valley a couple of miles to Dark Creek Road. A stout woman wearing a big, black cowboy hat waved at them from beside a mailbox painted like a little red barn. She pointed at a driveway half-hidden by overgrown bushes.

She didn't look anything like the slim young woman in the photograph.

As Jessa and her mother pulled up to the small barn she silently agreed with Jimmy that Dark Creek was nothing at all like the luxurious Arbutus Lane.

The barn might once have been red but now the paint was faded to a dusty brown. Four stalls opened onto a covered walkway which, in turn, was open to a small courtyard and parking area. A couple of horses stood behind the barn in small paddocks. A liver-coloured horse with a white blaze stood quietly in cross-ties in the walkway. A short, round woman was painting something on the horse's hooves.

"Hello there—are you the girl Jimmy was talking

about?" asked the woman in the cowboy hat as she walked up the driveway.

Jessa nodded.

"I'm Barbara Bailey—that's Babe in the crossties over there, and her owner, Marjorie." Marjorie looked up from the back hoof she was working on and gave a quick nod in Jessa's general direction. She looked old. Mrs. Bailey looked even older. She tucked a strand of grey hair under her hat. Jessa wondered if there was anyone more her age at this barn.

"Well, as Jimmy told you—I need help—and I have a spare stall. Three days a week after school you can help me do stalls and on weekends you can do the whole lot yourself. There are four horses here right now—with yours, five. We have room for six but I tell you I'm just getting too old to keep up with the work all on my own. The final straw was when I put my back out a couple of months ago— couldn't rest it properly so it took forever to heal.

If you're interested, the stall is yours. A recommendation from my boy, Jimmy is all I need. Your work will cover basic feed—hay, pellets, a little sweet feed—but, of course you're responsible for shoes, vet, trailering, and anything else extra."

Jessa turned to look at her mother who shrugged and nodded her agreement to the deal. Mrs. Bailey hardly took a breath before continuing on.

"Keep in mind, horses have got to be looked after, rain or shine, no matter whether you're sick or healthy. We've got a pretty basic operation here—

all the owners work or are retired. So, none of us are really up to doing it all ourselves. You'll get to know all the ladies soon enough. You'll need your own water bucket, feed tub, New Zealand rug—and don't bother calling Arthur What's-his-name because I won't have him on the place doing shoes—he's too growly with the horses—even with Jasmine."

When Mrs. Bailey said the name, "Jasmine," her voice softened and she pointed at a lovely chestnut mare standing with her head over the paddock fence, watching the visitors intently.

"Ohhh . . . Jasmine," she cooed. "Is Mumsy talking about you?"

The big, chestnut mare nickered softly and nodded her head. This was too much for Mrs. Bailey to bear. She left the conversation unfinished and walked away to talk to her horse.

"Hm," said Jessa's mother, "interesting woman. What do you think?"

Jessa didn't say anything for a moment. What on earth was she to make of the little barn? There was no riding ring and the facilities seemed pretty basic compared to Arbutus Lane. On the other hand, compared to where her poor pony was right now, stuck in the mud with no real barn at all—this was paradise.

"It's great," she said firmly.

"If you're up for all that work, I'll help with the extra expenses," her mother said. "We'll just have to tighten our belts a little, I suppose."

Jessa beamed at her mother and then gave her a big hug.

"Oooooh, Mumsies," she said, gently copying Mrs. Bailey's sing-song cooing. "Thank you. Thank you sooooo much."

Early Saturday morning, Jessa perched on the rail of a paddock fence at Dark Creek Stables. The barn was quiet. Mrs. Bailey had left after feeding the horses and turning them out.

"We can do stalls together later today after you've settled that horse of yours in. Put him in the small paddock by the mailbox when you're done with him," Mrs. Bailey had said, leaning out the open window of her huge, old brown car.

Jessa squinted as the sun rose higher in the sky. Every time she heard a vehicle go past on the main road, she strained to see if a truck and trailer were turning into the long driveway.

Finally, Rosa pulled up to the barn in her old pickup, a battered trailer attached behind. Rebel had arrived!

Jessa jumped down from her perch on the railing and ran to help Rosa unload.

"Hi there, Jessa—I brought you his saddle and bridle—they need cleaning but they fit him pretty good. Stand back—he practically unloads himself."

Jessa stood to the side and watched as Rebel slowly and carefully backed down the ramp of the trailer. He stopped quietly once he felt his feet firmly on the gravel and calmly surveyed his surroundings.

"He likes it here already," said Rosa with a broad wink. "I can tell. Here you go."

She pulled the lead shank from where it lay over Rebel's neck and handed it to Jessa.

"I'll grab his tack from the truck—I brought you a couple of brushes and a hoof-pick, too. I didn't know what you had already. Oh, and there's an old riding helmet on the front seat. If it fits, you can borrow it. Why don't you walk him around so he can get the kinks out of those cute little legs of his?"

Jessa turned Rebel around and led him down the driveway. He spotted Jasmine in her paddock, lifted his head and let out a loud whinny that made Jessa jump. At the end of the driveway, she and Rebel both spied a thick clump of juicy green grass.

"That looks good, doesn't it?" Jessa said.

Rebel looked at Jessa with soft, dark eyes. How could she resist? Rebel munched hungrily on the lush grass. As he ate, Jessa looked him over. He looked little better than the first time she had seen him.

After a few minutes Rosa joined them.

"He's an easy keeper. He doesn't need much grain unless you're working him a lot. I'll drive over to your mother's place and get her to sign the papers —just to let her know what you're responsible for."

Jessa nodded.

"I've left a list of numbers for you; his vet and farrier. I pinned a note up on the board in the tack room with the dates he was last wormed and had his shots. You should also think about joining a Pony Club. In the meantime, Mrs. Bailey will look after you two. I'm not too worried."

"You know Mrs. Bailey?"

Rosa looked surprised. "Everybody's heard of Mrs. B. She goes to a lot of local shows with that gorgeous warmblood mare of hers. They say that horse looks a lot like the one Jimmy McBride got his big break on."

Jessa looked back towards the barn. She could just see Jasmine's head peeking over her paddock gate. She wondered why Mrs. Bailey was so interested in having top quality horses when she wasn't exactly a candidate for international competition.

"I'd better get going," Rosa said and headed off to get her truck and trailer turned around.

A few minutes later she drove past and both Rebel and Jessa looked up.

Rosa waved cheerfully.

"Have fun, you two! I'll stop by and visit sometime!"

Jessa waved back and watched as the truck and trailer pulled out onto the road and drove off. The quiet of the country surrounded them as the sound of the truck faded away. Two small birds chirped and fluttered in the bushes and Rebel stopped his steady munching to listen for a moment, his ears pricked forward intently.

"Okay, Rebel. It's time for you to have a bath. Come on."

Jessa led her pony back to the barn. She tied Rebel securely to the fence. She found a bucket and a sponge in the tack room. She had brought a new bottle of shampoo from home. With all her equipment ready, she set to work.

"There's not much point in brushing you, is there?" she murmured as she started sponging soapy water on the muddy pony's neck. She scrubbed and scrubbed until her arms ached. Rivers of brown water flowed off his back and dripped in muddy trickles from his belly when she rinsed him with water from the hose.

Once she had scrubbed his mane and tail, she squirted shampoo right out of the bottle onto Rebel's back and started scrubbing all over again. Even his blaze got a good polishing.

Finally, after one last rinse, Jessa stood back to admire her work. Rebel, dripping wet, looked at her forlornly.

"It's okay. I'm done," she assured him.

Jessa toweled him off using the big old beach towels her mother had contributed to the "Clean Up Rebel" campaign.

As she rubbed a spot just behind his withers, Rebel sighed with pleasure and his lower lip began to quiver. Jessa laughed and rubbed harder. Rebel's lip quivered faster and he leaned into Jessa's massage. Finally, when he was more or less dried off, Jessa took a step back.

"Wow! You look great!"

Rebel's legs were evenly marked with jet black, his mane and tail were thick and shiny. His white blaze positively shone from his soft, brown face.

"Let's go for a ride, okay? That way you can dry off properly."

Quickly Jessa tacked Rebel up. No doubt about it,

the saddle and bridle were next in line for the clean-up treatment.

Rebel stood motionless as Jessa mounted up. Willingly, he responded as she nudged him forward with her legs. They rode off together down the driveway and started exploring the network of trails through the surrounding countryside.

By the time Jessa turned back into the driveway nearly two hours later, her legs were stiff and her backside hurt but she couldn't have been happier.

She and Rebel had walked and trotted past farms, riding stables, a golf course and a gravel quarry. Whether he was walking by the side of the road or trotting along a sheltered trail, he was always quiet and willing. His trot was smart and not uncomfortable and Jessa had quickly got the hang of switching diagonals every so often.

Jessa put on Rebel's halter and fastened him in the crossties. She hummed happily to herself as she started to untack him.

"Where have you been?" demanded Mrs. Bailey, appearing from around the end of the barn.

Jessa jumped.

"Out on a trail. . . ."

Mrs. Bailey was bright red.

"What do you mean, 'out on a trail'? No offense, young lady, but that was a pretty stupid thing to do!"

"But. . . ."

"No buts! This is a new horse! You don't know a thing about him. How does he react to trucks? Or cows? Or the gravel pit down the way?"

"He was really good," Jessa said, her voice quavering. She had never seen a grownup so angry.

"Damn good thing, he was good! Anything could have happened to you out there! I wouldn't have had a clue where to start looking. I was just coming into the tack room to call your mother! I have a good mind to send you and that horse of yours packing!"

"Oh, no!" said Jessa. "Please . . . I didn't know. I didn't think it would be. . . ."

"Damned right, you didn't think. Now, I love horses dearly, but I know they sure as anything aren't going to do your thinking for you! I can't afford to have some irresponsible kid who can't think helping me around here."

Mrs. Bailey wiped her mouth with the back of her hand. "Jeeez, you had me worried."

"I'm really sorry. But I thought a trail would be a good idea. And there's no ring. . . . And you weren't here so I couldn't tell you where I was going."

Jessa couldn't think what else to say. She had let Mrs. Bailey down, and Jimmy who had recommended her, and her mother who was counting on her to help earn her horse's keep. She didn't know what she would do if Mrs. Bailey changed her mind.

"I'm really, really sorry. I won't do that again, I promise. Please give me another chance."

Mrs. Bailey spat in the dirt. Jessa's eyes widened. She had never seen a woman spit before.

"Sorry I yelled. But I was really worried about you two. Now, here's the deal on trails. For the first two weeks you ride him up in the big field—no arguments. If he takes off on you, at least he can't go far. After that, you sign in and out on the chalk board in the tack room. Jot down the time you leave, where you're going, and when you'll be back. And, if you can, try to arrange to ride with someone when you're out on the trails. It's safer."

Jessa nodded gratefully. "Okay. Fair enough. Thanks, Mrs. Bailey."

"Hmph. Everyone deserves a second chance, I suppose," she said, and stalked up to the house.

Jessa heaved a huge sigh of relief. She and Rebel had arrived back just in time. It would have been even worse if Mrs. Bailey had phoned her mother.

When she came out of the tack room with Rebel's brushes he nickered at her softly.

"How did you know I had a carrot in my pocket?" she asked.

After Jessa had finished grooming Rebel, she turned him out into his paddock. He looked beautiful, his soft, brown coat shining in the sun.

He sniffed the ground and then, without a thought for all Jessa's hard work, he slowly sank to his knees and had a good roll in the dirt.

"Oh, Rebel, how could you?" groaned Jessa.

She couldn't stay angry for long. As soon as the pony had stood up and shaken himself off, he came to the fence and nuzzled her open hands. He gave her a lick and then ambled off to eat some of the hay Mrs. Bailey had left out for him.

With Rebel safely in his paddock, Jessa decided to get started on the stalls. She found a shovel and a wheelbarrow and set to work.

Jessa shoveled the mix of wood shavings and manure into the wheelbarrow. It was hard to believe one horse could make such a mess in just one night. She rested for a moment and noticed to her horror that Mrs. Bailey was standing in the stall door. Jessa blushed. *How long had she been watching her work?* she wondered. She could only imagine what Mrs. Bailey would have to say to her now.

"May I show you how to muck out a stall properly?" Mrs. Bailey asked.

Jessa looked at the half-full wheelbarrow. *What on earth had she done wrong now?* She offered Mrs. Bailey the shovel.

"I don't need that yet," she said and reached past Jessa for the purple manure rake. "Back in the old days when I was about your age, we used metal pitchforks," she said, deftly sweeping the tines of the plastic rake under a pile of droppings.

"Straw was a lot harder to deal with—although personally I like the look of a horse bedded down knee-deep in golden straw. Something romantic about that, don't you think?"

Jessa nodded and watched Mrs. Bailey give the rake a shake. A shower of dry wood chips sprinkled to the stall floor leaving only a small pile of droppings on the rake.

"Horse apples—great for the garden," Mrs. Bailey remarked.

With an expert flick, the horse apples flew across the stall and landed with a soft drum roll in the wheelbarrow. The curved, plastic tines of the manure rake quivered.

"Do you have any idea how much these shavings cost?"

Jessa shook her head. Mrs. Bailey didn't stop scooping and tossing long enough to notice. Jessa was glad she didn't have to contribute much to the conversation. Mrs. Bailey was on a roll and talked non-stop. Jessa wondered how long someone could talk about manure.

"Well, let me tell you—bedding isn't cheap. Which is why we shake off the dry stuff and use it as the first layer for the next day. Of course, these wet patches. . . ."

Mrs. Bailey exchanged the rake for the aluminum shovel and scraped a dark patch of shavings away to reveal a black rubber mat below.

". . . these wet patches . . . we take all this out— see how I'm scraping the shavings up? Not too hard, mind you—you'll shred the mat—any idea how much these rubber mats cost? Anyway, leave the stalls to air dry and then put the fresh bedding in right at the end of your chores."

Quite abruptly, Mrs. Bailey leaned the shovel against the stall wall and stared straight at Jessa.

"More than you bargained for, hmmm?"

Jessa coughed, caught off guard. That was exactly what she had been thinking. Of course, there was no way she was going to admit that to old Mrs.

Horse Apple. She picked up the manure rake and plunged it into the bedding. Sure, mucking out stalls was hard work, but Rebel was worth it.

Chapter Five

At school on Monday, all the talk was about horses.

"My horse arrived on Saturday," Jessa said, beaming at the other girls as they sat together at a big table in the lunchroom. She could hardly believe she finally had something to say to the horsey crowd.

"Where are you going to keep him?" asked Monika.

Jessa pushed aside an image of Monika leading her prancing horse out of his box stall at Arbutus Lane. "Dark Creek Stables," Jessa said.

"Dark Creek?" asked Rachel. "Isn't that the Old Lady Barn?" Several of the girls giggled.

"Oh yeah—that place owned by crazy old Mrs. Bailey?" asked Monika. "She's nuts! She kisses that horse of hers in public when they go to shows!"

"She's not crazy," protested Jessa. "The place is fine. Rebel is happy there."

"So, tell everyone else about this Rebel horse of yours," Cheryl said. She had already heard all the details on the phone, but she was quite eager to hear about Rebel again.

"He's great!" said Jessa, her enthusiasm returning, and launched into a long description of their weekend trail ride. She left out the part about Mrs. Bailey getting mad at her.

"Does he jump?" asked Rachel.

"What about his flatwork? How much schooling has he had?" asked Sarah Blackwater. The way she asked the question with her superior smirk, Jessa knew Sarah didn't think Rebel had much potential. Sarah was a perfectionist in just about everything she did—including riding.

Jessa had seen her practicing at Arbutus Lane. She would ride her three loop serpentines over and over again, not stopping until each curve was exactly even with the next.

"We're working on turns on the forehand right now, and leg-yielding—and of course, collection and extension at all three gaits," Sarah boasted. "I can't wait until we start on the Medium Level dressage tests. Anansi is really ready now—you should see his counter canter—it's so balanced. . . ."

"I guess it's hard to ride properly without a ring," said Rachel, interrupting her friend. Rachel wasn't nearly as interested in dressage as Sarah.

"Yeah, I guess old ladies don't need a ring," said Monika.

All the girls except Jessa laughed.

"Hey, lighten up, Jessa—we're just joking around," said Monika.

"Yeah, your little pony is probably really cute," added Rachel.

Sarah pulled a long printed sheet of paper out of her neatly organized binder. She snapped the rings shut and smoothed the paper flat on the table.

"Who else has their Arbutus Lane Spring Horse Show Forms yet?" she asked.

"Let's see!" said Rachel. All the girls gathered around to see the list of classes.

After much discussion, Jessa could see that no matter what she entered, she and Rebel wouldn't have a chance at any ribbons.

Of course, Sarah and Anansi were going to enter almost every flat class. Monika Jacobowski and her horse, Silver Dancer, were going to jump everything in sight, probably at breakneck speed.

"What are you taking Gazelle in, Rachel?" Monika asked.

"She's so green I'm going to take her in the First Year Combination Hunter Classic Series. That should be a good introduction for her. Of course, I'll move her up to harder classes later this season, when she's a little more comfortable." Jessa groaned inwardly at Rachel's false modesty. She and her super pony were far too advanced to enter such an easy set of classes.

Rachel pointed at a box which described the Hunter Classic Series.

"The first class is a hunter on the flat, the second is a working hunter class with a single jump at the end and then the last one is a hunter class over fences not to exceed 2' 6". They add up the points for each class and then the horse-and-rider combination with the most points wins a trophy and a leather halter with the horse's name engraved on it.

I've already seen the trophy. My dad donated it,"

she added smugly.

"Hey—I could enter that," said Monika.

"No you couldn't," said Rachel. "It also says this has to be the first year the horse and rider have been a combination. I've only been riding Gazelle for six months. You've been riding Silver for nearly two years now."

"Rebel and I are a first year horse-and-rider combination," said Jessa quickly, reaching for the entry form to get a better look.

"Well, no offense, but what about the class over fences? Does that pony of yours jump?" asked Rachel snatching the form back from Jessa.

Jessa glared at her. "Well, I'm not worried. We have lots of time to get ready. You'll just have to wait and see, won't you?" said Jessa, sounding a whole lot more confident than she felt.

"You'll be brilliant!" said Cheryl. "Do you have a groom yet?"

"A groom?" Rachel laughed and Jessa shot her a dirty look.

"Would you like to be my groom, Cheryl?" Jessa asked.

"I would be delighted to accompany you to the winner's circle."

"That's just in horse-racing," said Jessa.

"Whatever. I'll carry your trophy for you when you win the Classic Hunter Series."

"That's the Hunter Classic. You've got a deal. Can you come to my place after school?"

"Sure! That sounds like fun."

Jessa was glad Cheryl's big, loud voice was on her side.

Chapter Six

On Saturday morning, Jessa yawned and stretched lazily. All her homework was done and she was looking forward to spending the rest of the day at the stables. For two weeks she had diligently worked with Mrs. Bailey after school. Her stall-cleaning abilities had greatly improved. Mrs. Bailey had even commented on how well Jessa and Rebel seemed to get along.

Today was the first day Jessa was going back out on the trails. She could hardly wait! She galloped down the stairs and joined her mother at the breakfast table.

"Liz called this morning," her mother said. She wants to know if you can watch Bucky for a couple of hours later this afternoon. You know, it's supposed to rain today. Are you sure you want to go riding?"

Jessa's mother poured herself a cup of tea and spread the newspaper open on the kitchen table. Jessa groaned to herself. Bucky was four years old and lived next door with his mother, Elizabeth. His favourite game was sword fighting with old

Christmas paper wrapping tubes.

"Mom. It's less than a month until the show—I have so much to do with Rebel. I had already planned to work on our downward transitions today!"

Secretly, Jessa was glad the weather looked threatening. All week Mrs. Bailey had been promising to ride out with Jessa. If it was really miserable, maybe she wouldn't insist on coming along on the trail ride.

"Then I have to call Cheryl to see if she can come over. She should work on her leg bandaging technique. She can practice on me . . . or a chair leg or something. . . . Mom? Mom, are you listening to me?"

"Hmmmm?" Jessa's mother looked up from the paper. "Did you say something about a horse show?"

"Mom! I told you about the show! There are only three weekends between now and then and I haven't even jumped Rebel once! So that's why I don't have time to watch Bucky today."

"Watch your tone of voice, Miss Richardson."

"Sorry," Jessa grumbled. "But I really can't. Besides, it takes me two hours to do all the stalls and feed and. . . ."

"Well, I already told Liz you'd be happy to watch him for a couple of hours. Do your barn chores, go for a little ride, and then come straight home. Cheryl can still come over. She can practice bandaging Bucky's legs."

Jessa pushed her bangs out of her eyes in exasperation.

"You need a haircut."

"Mom!" Jessa pushed her chair away from the table and stomped upstairs to her room. Her mother just did not understand what it was going to take to get ready for the Arbutus Lane show. She also didn't understand how much she disliked looking after Bucky.

"Be back at four o'clock," her mother called up the stairs. Jessa didn't answer. She felt like slamming her door. Instead she shut it quietly and quickly got changed to go to the barn.

Half way to Dark Creek Stables, Jessa felt the first drops of rain on her cheeks. By the time she rode her bike up the driveway to the barn, she was soaking wet.

She pushed the bike into the open shed where the wood shavings were kept.

"Ugh," she groaned as she shook her wet hair.

Grey clouds pressed dark and solid against the horizon. Water streamed from the overhang of the shed roof like a wet wall between Jessa, the barn and her horse. Jessa sighed.

There wasn't much point in waiting for things to clear up. The rain was here to stay. Like her mom always said, Vancouver Island wouldn't be green all year round without all the rain. Somehow, as she tried to ignore the chill dribble of water down the back of her neck, Jessa didn't find greenery too inspiring. In fact, given a choice, California or Arizona seemed like good places to live.

Jessa found Rebel sheltering under the big cedar tree in his paddock.

When he saw her sloshing through the mud he lifted his head and pricked his ears forward. Jessa joined him under the great, ancient tree and pressed close against his warm, damp shoulder. He turned and nuzzled her gently. She fished in her pocket and found a piece of carrot. Rebel took the treat gently from her palm. His warm, moist breath blew over her chilled fingers. He sniffed at her hand, looking for more.

"Was that good?" she asked.

He bobbed his head up and down as if in agreement.

"You're so clever!" she said, and patted him on the neck.

She slipped the halter over his head and led him from the shelter of the tree. Together they crossed the courtyard to the barn.

"You get to go out on the trail today, you lucky boy."

In the tack room, Jessa found a note from Mrs. Bailey pinned to the board.

J-

Sorry I can't go out on the trail
ride—had to run into town.
If you still want to go, be careful.
Take a hoof pick with you.

B.B.

Jessa tucked a hoof pick into the back pocket of her jeans. Mrs. Bailey was such a worry wart. Rebel had been perfect that first day on the trail. Now, after two weeks of riding nearly every day in the big field, Jessa knew him even better. She jotted a quick note on the board letting Mrs. Bailey know how long she would be gone and the direction she was headed and went back out to Rebel where he stood quietly in the cross-ties.

Jessa toweled him off and groomed him as best she could. She saddled up quickly—partly because she was eager to ride, and partly because she was freezing.

In record time, Rebel was tacked up and Jessa was ready to go, rain cover on her helmet and rain slicker pulled down to cover as much of her legs and the saddle as possible.

The pair headed down the driveway through the potholes that had already turned to puddles.

"Some pleasure ride," moaned Jessa as she shortened her reins.

Rebel tensed slightly, waiting to see what was expected of him. Jessa put her legs firmly to his sides and urged him into a trot. Just like she had learned in her lessons, she drove him forward into the bit without letting him trot faster.

"Come on, Rebel—let's see your winning trot!"

Jessa felt Rebel's powerful haunches driving forward under her. His stride lengthened and his head stayed still and low, his neck arched and graceful.

Jessa kept her rising trot until she turned off the path at the side of the road and they entered the sheltered quiet of the Dark Creek Railway Trail. Rebel's trot slowed as he felt the fine, crushed gravel of the old railway bed underfoot.

Bushes and trees lined both sides of the wide trail. The rest of the world disappeared beyond the peaceful muted greenery of the lush corridor.

By the time Jessa had ridden ten minutes along the trail, both she and Rebel were soaking wet. Water still dribbled down her neck. She stopped for a minute and tried to adjust her riding helmet and rain slicker but no matter what she did, the water came in anyway.

"Forget it," she mumbled, shrugging her shoulders up around her ears and blowing warm air into her riding gloves.

Ignoring a small voice of caution inside her head, Jessa reached forward and patted Rebel's neck. "Okay, boy—how about a little canter?" She squeezed Rebel's sides. Willingly, her horse responded. They cantered along, splashing through the puddles. Jessa sat deep into the saddle and let Rebel's powerful stride take them steadily along the trail.

After a few minutes, Jessa asked Rebel to collect the canter. Again he responded as if the two of them had been riding together forever. He rounded his neck and shortened his stride. Jessa concentrated on her leg position as she thought through her aids for an extended canter. She was about to apply them when she saw another horse coming along the trail towards them.

Rebel spotted the horse and rider at the same time and his ears pricked forward. He whinnied loudly as Jessa slowed to a walk and strained to see through the rain. She couldn't quite make out who the other rider was.

The other horse was easier to see. A powerful black horse pranced towards them. The horse and rider seemed to float along without effort. Like a pair of perfectly matched dancers, they barely seemed to touch the ground with each light step.

The two riders drew closer to each other. She was quite surprised to see that the rider of the black horse was a boy not much older than herself. She was even more surprised when he smiled and waved a greeting.

"Hi! Is this your new horse?" he asked.

Jessa pulled Rebel to a halt and looked hard at the boy. It suddenly dawned on her where she had seen him before.

"Oh, hi! Jeremy, right? I didn't recognize you with your helmet on."

The boy nodded.

"This is my horse, Caspian."

"He's gorgeous," said Jessa.

"Only the serious riders are out today," Jeremy said, smiling at Jessa. "Are you heading for the indoor ring at the Equestrian Centre?"

Jessa glanced along the trail. She didn't want to admit she couldn't afford the monthly ring rental fee.

"Ummm . . . no. It's a bit far to ride there from here . . . and, ummm . . . I like working on the trail."

"Hey! You are the first person I've met who likes working outside a ring! I like it better than being stuck in a ring."

"You do?" Jessa couldn't hide the surprise in her voice. *Why would anyone practice out in the pouring rain if they had a choice?*

"I think the horses are much happier training out on the trail," Jeremy went on. "It keeps their minds occupied and they don't get ring sour and bored."

"Oh, right. For sure," agreed Jessa. Feeling more confident, she started, "We're trying to get ready for the. . . ." Just as suddenly she felt foolish and stopped. Looking at Caspian and Jeremy she realized she would be completely outclassed at the Classic.

"We're getting ready for a little schooling show at . . . at. . . ."

Thankfully, Jeremy interrupted.

"Why don't you enter the Spring Classic at the Equestrian Centre? That's what we're getting ready for. Right, Caspian?" He slapped Caspian on the neck.

"I . . . I'm not really sure that we're ready . . ." Jessa said.

"Oh, don't worry. Neither are we. I haven't shown Caspian anywhere yet this year. The show will have classes for all levels, you know. I hope I'll see you there. . . ."

"I . . . I don't know . . ." Jessa mumbled awkwardly.

"Your horse looks like he works really well for you."

Jessa swallowed and looked down at Rebel's shoulder. She suddenly felt very strange, as if she couldn't trust herself to speak properly.

"He's pretty good," she nodded. "Nothing like yours, of course."

Jeremy leaned forward to scratch Caspian behind the ears.

"Do you like jumping?" he asked.

In her mind, Jessa saw herself flying over the neck of her school horse, Benji, the summer before when he hit the brakes right before a small oxer.

"Yeah, sure!" It wasn't exactly a lie. She liked jumping. She just wasn't very good at it.

"Have you done the log yet?"

Jeremy gestured back along the trail.

"Log? What log?" Jessa asked. She couldn't remember seeing any logs lying around.

Before she could protest, Jeremy wheeled Caspian around and urged him into a canter. Even if Jessa had tried to stop him, Rebel had ideas of his own. A fast canter along a muddy trail with another horse looked like great fun to him!

He snorted and leaped forward into a fast canter, and then a gallop, pounding along the trail to catch up to Caspian.

"Oh, no," gasped Jessa.

She grabbed a fistful of mane and let Rebel navigate the mud and puddles. Water and mud splashed her face as they drew closer behind Jeremy and Caspian.

"Don't let me fall off, please don't let me fall off . . ." she whispered. Her words escaped into the rain.

Jeremy glanced over his shoulder to see where Jessa was. A broad grin flashed across his face. He crouched lower over Caspian's neck and urged his horse on.

"Oh, no . . ." groaned Jessa.

Her heart pounded and the wind brought tears to her eyes as they tore along the trail faster and faster.

The leafy bushes along the trail whipped past in a green blur. Rebel's breath came in quick snorts with each galloping stride.

Jessa hung on for dear life, half horrified and half exultant. She couldn't tell whether the expression on her face was a grimace of terror or a big smile.

She heard Jeremy shout something, but the words were lost in the thunder and splash of their horses' hooves.

He sat up and pulled Caspian to a slow canter, then a trot. Rebel pranced and tossed his head as he, too, slowed down.

"He's pretty fast for a little guy!" Jeremy said, laughing and out of breath.

Steam rose from the horses' necks as they walked side by side through the drizzle.

"We'll have to be careful or we'll miss the turn-off," Jeremy said.

On her previous outing, Jessa hadn't noticed a place to leave the main trail. Even though she scanned the path ahead carefully, she would have ridden right past the small gap beside an old cedar tree if Jeremy hadn't led the way.

"Watch your head!"

Jeremy needn't have said anything. Rebel followed Caspian under the low branches of the great old tree. Jessa had no choice but to lean forward and press her cheek against his wet neck.

A narrow path wound between thick bushes. Jessa gave Rebel his head and he picked his way over fallen branches and uneven ground. Caspian slithered down a low bank to a creek and splashed right through and up the other side. Not wanting to be left behind by his new companion, Rebel quickly followed.

On the far side of the creek the path widened a little. In a few minutes they emerged in a grassy clearing. An old oak tree had fallen across the middle of the clearing. Jeremy stopped and surveyed the obstacle.

"There are two ways to jump it," he said. He pointed at the middle of the tree. "The middle is actually easier to jump, even though it's a little higher, because the approach is better."

Jessa eyed the fallen tree with horror. *Surely he didn't mean that she should try to jump it?* The way the middle of the trunk was propped up on a sturdy branch, Rebel would have to clear at least three feet! Jessa had never jumped anything higher than about eighteen inches in her class and even those jumps had given her trouble at times.

She thought again of the oxer and the day she had sailed over her Benji's shoulder and landed on the jump. If that had been painful and embarrassing, a fall here in the clearing, with Jeremy and his wonder horse watching, would be even worse!

Jeremy was oblivious to her reluctance. He was still describing her options.

"If you jump at this end, you have to come at it after a quick turn—and these twiggy branches make it seem bigger. Caspian hates the take-off and always jumps huge. So, what do you think?"

Jessa didn't answer. She pretended to be studying the middle of the jump. She couldn't think how on earth she was going to get out of this one. Her opportunity to come up with a believable excuse disappeared when Jeremy turned Caspian in the clearing, clucked twice and picked up a strong trot. Jeremy went straight into two-point and Caspian bounced easily over the middle of the oak tree. They landed smoothly and cantered off into a space in the brush on the other side of the clearing.

Jessa tried to hold Rebel back but when he saw the black horse disappear, he took matters into his own hands and cantered after him. Unfortunately, the quickest route was right over the middle of the fallen oak tree.

Jessa didn't even have time to cry out. Rebel gathered himself and leaped over the big log. Jessa lunged forward onto his neck. One foot flew out of the stirrup and she felt herself sliding to the side as he headed for the opening in the bushes where the trail continued. Jessa struggled to keep her balance. Somehow, she managed to pull herself back into the saddle.

She was so busy trying not to lose her reins, she hardly noticed as a thin branch whipped across her cheek, cutting her slightly. Abruptly, Rebel stopped, nearly unseating her again.

From the other side of another clearing, much smaller than the one they had just left, Caspian lifted his head from where he was grazing and nickered softly. Quickly, Jessa sat up straight and took a deep breath. She looked behind her at the thickly screened path from which she had just emerged and realized with relief that Jeremy couldn't see the jump from where he was waiting.

"That was fun!" she said, hoping he wouldn't notice the quaver in her voice. She let Rebel put his head down so he, too, could enjoy a bit of grass. Her hands shook as the reins slid through them.

Jeremy looked at her. "Are you okay?"

"Yeah . . . sure. . . ."

"Your cheek!"

Jessa put her hand up to her cheek. When she drew her fingers away, they were smudged with blood.

"Here." Jeremy jumped off Caspian and handed Jessa a paper napkin. She pressed it to her cheek.

"Thank you."

"Lucky I stopped for a burger on my way to the barn or I wouldn't have had that in my pocket."

Seeing the horrified look on Jessa's face he added, "don't worry—I didn't use that one!"

Jessa smiled. On top of having a great horse, Jeremy seemed really nice.

"I'm fine, really," she said, dabbing her cheek. "It doesn't even hurt."

Jeremy smiled at her and got back on his horse. He looked at his watch.

"Well, we should be off or we'll never get to the beach."

"The beach?" Jessa couldn't imagine what they would get up to at the beach.

"To do circles and serpentines. They're a little hard to do on narrow trails."

"How do you get to the beach?"

Jeremy pointed back towards the main trail. "You take the railway trail to that little road by the chicken farm and then you get to this other small trail by the golf course . . . I'll show you. . . ."

Jessa flushed. She didn't feel like suffering another riding embarrassment at the beach. There wouldn't be many bushes to hide behind down there. She didn't want Jeremy to see her do egg-shaped circles and pointy serpentines.

"That would be great," she said. "But I don't really have time today."

"No problem. Can I phone you so we can plan to ride down there together?"

"Ummm . . . sure . . . I guess. I mean, that would be great!" Jessa stumbled, suddenly embarrassed all over again, though this time she wasn't quite sure why.

"I can get your phone number from Rachel—I don't have a pen with me and I'll never remember it until I get back to the barn."

Jeremy looked down at the steam rising off Caspian's glossy wet haunches.

"We'd better go—I'm getting cold. Are you sure you're okay?"

Jessa nodded. "I think it's stopped bleeding."

Jeremy looked awkward for a moment and then checked his watch again.

"Okay . . . well—we're off."

"Thanks. I mean, I'll see you," she said.

Jeremy touched his heels to Caspian who stepped off lightly and then picked up a lovely collected trot.

This time, Jessa was ready. She held Rebel firmly and steered him slowly around the uprooted end of the oak tree as they crossed the clearing on the way back to the main trail. By the time she turned Rebel back towards home, Caspian and Jeremy were out of sight. She could hear their retreating hoofbeats fade away around a curve in the trail.

She encouraged Rebel to move on and he set off through the rain towards the barn. Jessa heaved a deep sigh. The soft rain falling on the fresh new leaves was cool, soothing. She wished she never had to go back.

A small brown rabbit hopped out into the middle of the trail. It froze and stared hard at Jessa and Rebel, almost defying them to keep going.

Jessa smiled. A horse and rider must seem huge to such a tiny creature.

Are you going to let us run you over? she asked silently. But the rabbit had no intention of being stepped on. At the last possible moment it darted back into the bushes and disappeared with hardly a rustle.

Rebel calmly continued on his way, his rider's thoughts reluctantly turning to games a four-year-old might enjoy playing.

Chapter Seven

"So then, we jumped over the big tree," Jessa said excitedly over lunch in the school cafeteria.

"Yeah, right," said Rachel. "There aren't any logs on the Railway Trail."

"For your information, Jeremy showed me this secret little path—you really have to look for it or you'd ride right past."

Rachel looked disgusted. Jessa ignored her and continued to recount her adventures.

"Then, when I was cantering through this narrow part of the little trail, a branch scratched my cheek and he was so nice and worried. . . ."

"You're soooo lucky," crooned Sarah. "Did you see him ride?"

"Of course," grinned Jessa. "I was right behind Caspian when we galloped along the Railway Trail."

"Galloped?" asked Bridget. "You galloped with Jeremy?"

All the girls except Rachel looked at Jessa in awe. Rachel stabbed viciously at a french fry and scowled.

"What about the jump?" asked Monika.

"Rebel flew over it! He's such a good horse." Jessa grinned at the other girls.

"Pony," corrected Rachel coolly.

"Rachel! A mere technicality!" Cheryl quickly came to Jessa's defense.

Rachel didn't answer. She glared at Jessa, picked up her tray and stalked off to sit at a different table. The girls watched her leave in silence.

"What's *her* problem?" Cheryl asked finally.

Jessa shrugged and shook her head.

"Come on, we'd better go and see what's wrong," said Monika, nodding in Rachel's direction. She and Sarah picked up their trays and walked across the cafeteria to join Rachel.

As the girls sat down, Rachel leaned over and whispered something in Sarah's ear. Sarah glanced over at Jessa and then quickly looked away again. She shook her head, said something quietly, and all three girls laughed.

"Okay, now that they're gone, are you going to tell me what's going on?" asked Cheryl.

"Nothing. I have no idea what their problem is," insisted Jessa.

"Come on," said Cheryl. "Let's go sit by the window. I think I'll puke if I have to watch those three any longer."

As soon as Jessa and Cheryl were settled at their new table, Cheryl leaned over. "Okay, now you can tell me what *really* happened."

"What?" Jessa wondered if all her friends had lost their minds.

Cheryl looked hurt. She put her hands on her hips and pushed out her bottom lip. "I thought I was your best friend?"

"Look. I have no idea what you are talking about."

"Oh, come on. The whole school knows. You're lucky I don't get hurt feelings easily. I can't believe you didn't tell me!"

"Tell you what?"

"As if you didn't know." Cheryl tutted in disgust.

"This isn't funny any more. What are you talking about?" Jessa felt tears pricking at the back of her eyelids. *Why was everyone picking on her?* "Maybe I should just go and sit somewhere by myself."

Cheryl looked long and hard at Jessa.

"You really don't know?"

Jessa shook her head.

"Wow. Well, for your information, Jeremy Digsby, super horseman, is in love with you."

"What!" Jessa coughed and sputtered as some of her orange juice went down the wrong way.

"He's asking everyone for your phone number!"

"What!" Jessa gasped between coughs.

"Well, that's what Rachel says."

"What!" Jessa's eyes watered as she started choking again. Cheryl slapped her on the back.

"Ow! Stop. I'm . . . I'm fine, I'm fine now." Between gasps for breath Jessa sputtered, "he is not in love with me! He just wants to take me to the beach!"

"Oooooh! It *is* serious!" Cheryl's eyes flashed with delight. "How romantic!"

"No! It's not like that. He trains his horse down there. It was a total accident! We ran into each other on the trail—that's all. I don't understand why anyone cares."

"Think about it," said Cheryl, leaning forward so nobody else could hear. "You know Rachel is crazy about Jeremy."

"So?"

"I bet he's never phoned her to invite her to go to the beach."

"That's just because she probably doesn't ride in the rain," protested Jessa.

Now it was Cheryl's turn to look confused. "What?"

"Oh, never mind."

"Isn't it obvious that Rachel's jealous? Look at her, she's as green as her jello!"

Jessa looked over at Rachel who was carefully keeping her back turned to them.

"Do you really think so?"

Cheryl nodded gravely. "Of course. You'd better watch your back."

"But I didn't do anything!"

"That doesn't matter. She thinks you did."

Jessa picked at the edge of her slice of pizza. She wasn't hungry any more. She hoped Jeremy would forget to call, that he would forget he had ever seen her on the trail.

Later that afternoon Jessa swerved her bike around a pothole in the driveway at Dark Creek

Stables. Cheryl whooped as she rode straight through the puddle.

Cheryl was taking her responsibilities as Rebel's personal groom very seriously. Each day after school she raced through her homework with Jessa, and then the two girls rode their bikes to the barn.

Rebel soon knew when to expect them and was always waiting by the gate of his paddock.

Between the two of them it took almost no time at all to help Mrs. Bailey finish cleaning the stalls and to put feed and water out for each horse.

As soon as the girls had Rebel ready, they all set off down the trail—Rebel and Jessa in front and Cheryl pedaling her bike slowly behind.

"Keep your heels down," Cheryl shouted. "Look up! Sit deep in the saddle!"

Cheryl was no longer happy just giving advice on tail braiding and clipping whiskers. She had been reading lots of horse books and had appointed herself Jessa's personal coach.

"You'll never win the Classic if you bounce around like that!"

On Friday, Cheryl stayed overnight at Jessa's house.

"I might as well move in here, Mrs. Richardson," she joked with Jessa's mother when Jessa and Cheryl walked in after school. They all laughed.

"So, let me guess, what are you girls doing tomorrow?"

Cheryl let out a very loud whinny and stomped her feet under the table.

Jessa giggled and her mother rolled her eyes.

"Don't talk too late tonight so you can get an early start in the morning. Remember, you promised to watch Bucky tomorrow afternoon."

"Do I have to?" Jessa asked, even though she already knew what her mother would say. "We have to do all the barn chores in the morning."

"Yes, you have to. I don't want to have another argument like last week. Besides, Liz is going to pay you for baby-sitting and I'd like you to save enough over the next couple of weeks to pay your own entry fees in that show."

"I'll make sure she gets back in time, don't worry," said Cheryl. "I don't mind helping Jessa. I kind of like mucking out. And you know how good I am with little kids."

Cheryl smiled sweetly at Jessa's mother. Jessa couldn't help being a bit annoyed. Surely her mother could see right through her friend's little act. Jessa didn't think Cheryl liked baby-sitting any more than she did.

Mrs. Richardson smiled gratefully. "Thanks, Cheryl. I'll order pizza in tonight and then you girls can watch a video. Just remember—straight to sleep after the movie."

"Oh, great!" said Cheryl. "Thanks!"

"Yeah, thanks," mumbled Jessa.

When the alarm rang at eight the next morning, both girls were still sound asleep. Jessa groped in the general direction of the alarm clock.

"Turn that thing off!" Cheryl moaned. Jessa found the snooze button and the room was quiet again. Sun streamed in through the window. Outside somewhere, Jessa heard the whine of a lawn-mower.

When the alarm went off again ten minutes later, Cheryl sat up with a loud groan. Jessa rolled over and burst out laughing.

"Your hair! It's sticking straight up!"

Cheryl put her hand up to her head and ruffled through her thick, red hair. She stuck her tongue out at Jessa. "Where are my glasses?"

Jessa handed them to her, put on her own and then turned off the alarm.

"Yuck. I can't stand that noise. It reminds me of school!"

"Does the word 'manure' inspire you to action?" asked Cheryl.

"No . . . but the words 'Hunter Classic' do," Jessa answered.

Both girls jumped out of bed and trotted downstairs for breakfast.

"Hey! What's this?"

Jessa turned Rebel around and rode back to where Cheryl was standing beside her bike pointing at something at the side of the trail.

"What's what?" she asked.

Cheryl pulled some tall grass aside to reveal a colourful hand-painted sign.

"What does it say?" Jessa asked.

"Rainbow Adventure Trail. Where do you think it goes?"

"It doesn't look much like a trail to me," answered Jessa. She looked doubtfully at the over-grown path where Cheryl was already trying to push her bike.

"It wouldn't be much of an adventure if it were paved, would it?" said Cheryl as she disappeared from sight.

"Wait for us!" Jessa called and encouraged Rebel to push his way through the tall grass and bushes. She squinted her eyes shut as branches snapped at her. Rebel put his head down and kept going.

"We're not the first ones to come through here," Cheryl called back from somewhere ahead.

"How can you tell?" asked Jessa, dodging branches as they clutched at her legs.

"There are hoof prints along here."

"You're kidding!" Jessa shouted back.

Jessa ducked under a low branch. Rebel stopped, eyed a particularly thick clump of bushes and then plowed on.

"You must think we're crazy," Jessa whispered reassuringly.

"Did you hear that?" called Cheryl.

"Hear what?"

"That noise!"

"What noise?"

"Be quiet and listen!"

Jessa halted Rebel and he immediately took advantage of the break to snatch a mouthful of greenery. Jessa couldn't hear anything except his loud munching.

A moment later, Cheryl pushed her way back through the bushes and appeared in front of them. She was walking, her bike nowhere in sight. She held a weathered piece of wood out in front of her. She turned it over in her hands and studied the back side of it.

"Is it ever thick in here," Jessa said. "Who would have come through here on a horse?" asked Jessa.

Cheryl shrugged and held the faded plank up for Jessa to see. "Look what I found lying under a tree. I think it must have fallen off—see—the wood's all rotten around the nail hole."

D   GER — BRIDGE O T

"What's that supposed to mean?" Half the letters were so faded Jessa couldn't read them. Cheryl peered more closely at the writing.

"'Danger! Bridge out!' I think that's what it's supposed to say," concluded Cheryl.

"What bridge?" Jessa asked. "There's no bridge back here. . . ."

"Shhhh!" interrupted Cheryl. "Did you hear it that time?"

"Hear what?"

"Someone was calling for help."

"Don't kid around," said Jessa. "There's nobody else back here."

"I heard it. I'm telling you—somebody's in trouble."

"Where did you leave your bike?"

"Up ahead. Come on, we have to go find whoever that is."

"You are hearing things."

Cheryl looked put out. "No I'm. . . ."

Both girls froze. Jessa felt all the hairs on her arms stand on end. This time, there was no mistaking the cry of pain and fear. From ahead in the bushes someone was calling, half moaning, half crying.

"Please! Help me! Help!"

Chapter Eight

Jessa and Cheryl looked at each other, eyes opened wide.

"What are we going to do?" asked Jessa, her mouth dry and her heart pounding.

Before Cheryl could answer, Rebel jerked his head up and listened intently. Suddenly he let out a loud whinny and both girls jumped.

"Rebel!"

Not too far ahead came an answering whinny and then a girl's voice calling again, more clearly now.

"Is somebody there? Please, come and help me!"

Cheryl turned and ran back through the bushes calling out as she went. "Where are you? Call again!"

"Over here at the old bridge! Hurry! Oh, help!"

Jessa and Rebel followed as quickly as they could, listening for the sound of the two voices calling back and forth to each other.

Rebel pushed his way into a clearing and Jessa pulled him up short. Cheryl was standing at one edge of an ancient wooden foot bridge. On the bridge a white horse lay on its chest and stomach. At first, Jessa couldn't tell what had happened.

A girl was kneeling at the horse's head, sobbing.

Cheryl's voice was small and scared. "The horse's legs went right through the rotted wood of the bridge. How are we going to get it out?"

Jessa jumped off Rebel and slowly walked forward, leading him behind her.

"Easy, Rebel," she said as the white horse raised its head from the bridge and looked back over its shoulder to watch their approach. Jessa joined Cheryl at the edge of a steep creek bank so she could see better.

The horse's legs hung stiffly beneath the bridge. Pieces of crumbled, rotten planks lay in the creekbed below. The horse's entire weight rested on a single large supporting log which ran along the middle of the underside of the bridge. From what Jessa could see, the horse must have just placed all four feet squarely on the narrow bridge when the rotting cross planks had crumbled under its weight.

Jessa swallowed hard. She didn't want to think about what would happen if that main support log gave way.

What sort of a fool would try to take a horse across such a rickety old bridge?

The girl on the bridge looked up. With a start, Jessa recognized the tear-streaked face and tumble of dark curls which spilled out from under the riding helmet.

"Rachel," Jessa whispered. "Rachel—are you okay?"

"What am I going to do? Poor Gazelle! She's going to die!"

Jessa looked down into the dry rocky creekbed about twelve feet below. If what remained of the bridge collapsed, there was no way that Gazelle could escape without a broken leg, or worse.

"Maybe you should get off the bridge," suggested Jessa, "while someone goes for help."

"She panics when I move! I can't leave her! I was leading her across and there was a big cracking sound and she freaked out and. . . ."

Rachel started sobbing again and buried her face in Gazelle's mane. The mare's laboured breathing was loud in the quiet clearing.

"We'd better go and get help," Cheryl said.

"No!" Rachel cried. "Don't go! It could collapse any minute!"

Both girls looked helplessly at the stricken pair in front of them.

"Please don't leave me here," she sobbed. "I don't want to die alone."

"You are not going to die and neither is your horse," said Cheryl decisively. Jessa was impressed with her friend's confident, calming voice. Inside, Jessa's stomach clenched. She didn't think she could be as cool and collected as Cheryl. She could hardly believe what Cheryl said next.

"I'm going to take Rebel and get help. You're better with horses, Jessa. You stay here with Rachel and see if you can keep Gazelle calm until I get back."

"But . . ." Jessa said. She didn't want to be left behind. *What would happen if the bridge gave way and Rachel fell onto the rocks far below?*

"No buts. I've been watching you ride Rebel. He's good. And don't forget—I did go to riding camp last year."

"But. . . ."

"Don't argue! There's no time. Give me your riding helmet. If I ride Rebel, I can cut across the field and go straight to the farm on the other side of the Railway Trail. My bike would never make it through the mud."

There was something in Cheryl's tone which made it impossible to disagree. The next thing Jessa knew she was giving her friend a leg up and watching her ride away through the bushes.

A sob from Rachel drew her attention back to the stranded mare on the bridge. Even lying so awkwardly on the bridge, Jessa was struck by how pretty Gazelle was. When Jessa took a step closer, Gazelle raised her head and watched her warily. Foam flecked her neck and Jessa could see the white of her eye.

"It's okay, girl," Jessa murmured.

"Jessa?" asked Rachel, her voice shaky.

"What?"

"Please come here and help me hold her head down. If she can't toss it maybe we can stop her from. . . ."

As if listening to the conversation, the beautiful arab mare threw her head back and tried desperately to free herself from her trap. Jessa stood transfixed with helpless horror. The mare's mane tossed and her muscles strained as she struggled frantically.

"Rachel?" Jessa called. "Are you okay?" Panic rose in Jessa's throat as she looked on, her hands reaching forward uselessly.

Rachel didn't answer. She concentrated only on her horse. "Steady. Whoa. . . ." After what seemed like ages, the horse stopped her wild thrashing and lay her head back down on the bridge beside Rachel.

Jessa watched in horror. The bridge was hardly wide enough for Rachel and her horse. Rachel's perch at her horse's head looked awfully precarious to Jessa. She wasn't sure how she would even get to Gazelle's head.

Gazelle's flanks heaved and with each breath she groaned. She had managed to move herself slightly forward but her legs remained trapped, hanging through the rotten bridge.

"Jessa, come and help me," pleaded Rachel. "I might not be able to hold her next time."

The desperate helplessness in Rachel's voice compelled Jessa to move closer. Cautiously she stepped onto the bridge. There was an ominous creak as her weight was added to the already strained structure.

Please don't let it collapse, she thought. Carefully she inched her way along the very edge of the bridge, trying to give the frightened horse as much room as possible.

She wished there was some sort of railing to hold onto. She glanced down to the dry, rocky creekbed far below and swallowed hard.

Jessa felt dizzy when she looked down, just like when she had climbed onto the roof of the garage to retrieve her frisbee. At least then she had been able to lie flat and hold onto something. She inched her way forward. When she was level with Gazelle's withers she stopped.

"Should I come over to your side?" she whispered, her heart racing.

"No. Just move forward a bit more so you can reach her head."

Jessa crept forward another foot. Very slowly she started to crouch down beside Gazelle.

This was too much for the terrified mare to stand. She threw her head backwards again and struggled wildly. She wrenched the reins from Rachel's hand and lunged up and forward.

Rachel shrieked and scrambled backwards out of the way, just managing to reach the safety of the far bank.

"Jessa!" she screamed.

But Jessa had no time to react. The mare's front hooves rose free above the bridge. As they broke loose one of them caught Jessa on the shoulder.

There was no time to cry out. No railing to reach for. Nothing to do but feel herself falling, falling, falling towards the creekbed below. Jessa felt as if she were moving in slow motion.

She seemed to hang in the air forever, long enough that Jessa wondered why she had given her helmet to Cheryl when she was the one falling.

Long enough to wonder if she'd be home in time to watch Bucky.

The smash as she landed on the dry boulders jerked her back into real time.

"Oh my God! Jessa! Jessa! Are you okay?"

Jessa tried to answer but only a whisper squeezed out of her. She couldn't breathe. She tried desperately to suck in a breath. Pain shot through her left arm and a thousand terrified thoughts flew through her head.

Was her back broken? Her arm? Had she smashed her ribs? Why couldn't she breathe?

She closed her eyes and a new horror flashed through her mind. *What if the bridge collapsed and the horse and the giant log fell on top of her?* She felt barely alive after the fall. She would never survive being crushed.

Jessa forced herself to ignore the pain and sucked in a shallow breath. She managed a little gasp. And then another. Then she opened her eyes.

She tried not to listen to Rachel's hysterical screaming and surveyed the situation from her position in the creekbed below the bridge.

Gazelle had managed to free her forelegs and these now hung over the side of the bridge. The horse's knees were hooked over a smaller log which supported the ends of the rotting cross-planks which had once made up the roadbed of the bridge.

How on earth had she managed to twist around like that?

90

From her vantage point Jessa could see that the horse's body was now resting on the main supporting log. If Gazelle struggled and her haunches slipped off that log, she would fall backwards right through the bridge. Jessa couldn't see how Gazelle could survive—either she would hang herself if her bridle got caught, or break her neck.

If, somehow, she managed to struggle free and came over the front edge of the bridge, she would probably break at least one foreleg, if something wasn't already broken.

"Be quiet!" Jessa finally managed to gasp. Rachel stopped crying for a minute.

"Are you okay! I thought you were dead!"

Jessa didn't answer. Rachel started sobbing again. Jessa tried to think how to best move out of the way. As it was, if Gazelle came off the bridge in any direction, she was going to land right on top of her.

Jessa tried to remember fourth grade health class when the paramedics had come to demonstrate first aid techniques. All she could remember was that you never put a tourniquet on a neck wound and never moved anyone with a possible back injury.

Jessa looked up and saw the desperate look in Gazelle's eyes. Under the circumstances, Jessa decided she didn't have too many options. Very carefully she moved first one foot and then the other. She wiggled all her toes.

She could breathe a little more easily now. Her left arm, the one she had landed on, throbbed with every terrified heartbeat. Even slightly moving her fingers sent a stab of pain shooting straight up through her left shoulder. Trying to bend her wrist brought stinging tears to her eyes.

Jessa's right shoulder, the one where Gazelle had kicked her when she lashed out in her panic, was numb and would hardly move at all.

Forcing herself to ignore the pain, she managed somehow to pull herself along the ground. She pushed cautiously with her feet and feeling like she was in a bizarre dream where all movement was agonizingly slow, inched her way to the side of the creekbed. A heavily overgrown, steep bank made it impossible to go any farther but at least she managed to move herself out of harm's way.

"What are we going to do?" whispered Rachel, looking down into the dry creekbed.

"Just stay quiet and wait for Cheryl to come back. And stay off the bridge." Jessa heard the abruptness in her own voice as if someone else had spoken the sharp words.

For a long time neither girl said anything. Jessa concentrated on lying perfectly still. Every now and then she wiggled her toes just to make sure she still could. Her arm throbbed and her back hurt.

"My dad is going to kill me," Rachel said softly and started to cry again.

"Rachel—stop crying. You have to stay calm. Just do me a favour and shut up." Jessa's words sounded unreal to her. *How could she expect Rachel to stay calm? Besides, she was probably right. Her father was going to be furious.*

A few minutes later the girls heard voices.

"They're just up ahead at that old bridge!"

Cheryl! Jessa nearly burst into tears with relief.

Three men carrying ropes, a long plank and shovels appeared at the edge of the creek bank. One of the men also had a rifle.

"Are you okay down there?" he called down to Jessa.

"I'll be okay," she said uncertainly, her voice quavery and weak. "Get the horse free."

The men consulted briefly. Jessa couldn't hear what they were saying but she could tell by the sound of their voices that they were worried.

One of them took a step towards the stranded horse and Gazelle panicked again. Looking up underneath the bridge Jessa saw the horse's powerful back legs kick back and down. At the same time, the mare threw her head and neck forward in a final desperate attempt to free herself.

There was a loud sound of splitting wood and Gazelle heaved herself forward, kicked clear of the bridge and launched herself into the air. Jessa closed her eyes and heard a crash and clatter as Gazelle landed in the creekbed.

In the silence which followed the horse's leap for freedom, Jessa held her breath and waited for the sound of a gunshot. But nothing happened.

"By God, will you look at that!" she heard one of the men say.

Cautiously, she opened her eyes and saw Gazelle munching on green grass growing at the foot of the bank on the far side of the creek. Rachel scrambled down through the thick tangle of underbrush and went to her horse. Gently she ran her hand down each of the mare's legs in turn.

"She's all scraped up but I think she's okay!" she called up to the others, disbelief and shock in her voice.

Jessa closed her eyes in relief. She leaned back and rested her head against a tree root. It was only then that she began to cry.

Chapter Nine

"There's someone here to see you, Jessa."

Jessa opened her eyes. For a moment she couldn't think where she was or why there was a nurse standing over her bed.

"Your friend is here to see you. Wake up."

The memories of the previous day's trip to the emergency room flooded back. They had prodded and poked for hours and sent her for X-rays three different times; head, chest, arm.

Even though the investigation only uncovered severe deep bruising and a badly sprained wrist, her doctor decided it would be wise to keep her in the hospital overnight.

"You can't be too careful in a case like this . . . trauma . . . possible head injury . . . painkillers . . . observation."

Jessa had been able to catch only snatches of the doctor's conversation which had taken place in the hallway just outside the emergency examining room.

The painkillers had been strong and Jessa didn't even remember moving from the emergency room into the bed where she was now lying.

"Where's my mom?" Jessa asked the nurse, taking the warm facecloth the nurse offered. She winced when she reached forward. There was no part of her body which didn't hurt. Her left arm was wrapped in a bandage and was tied across her stomach in a white gauze sling.

"Your mother is down in the cafeteria. She was starving. I told her you'd be fine. She insisted on staying with you last night. She slept in that chair! We were busy—your neighbor over there fell off a shed roof and broke her ankle."

Jessa looked over at the next bed. She couldn't see anything but a cast sticking out from under the blanket.

"It was a full house last night—two appendixes—that's unusual—we didn't have any more cots left for parents! Now, are you ready for visitors in a minute?"

The nurse didn't seem able to talk without doing something with her hands. She patted the sheet into place where it had come un-tucked, raised the head of the bed and wheeled the bed-table over so Jessa could reach it. She took Jessa's wrist between her thumb and two fingers. The nurse looked at a watch which hung upside-down from her name-tag. Her name was Rani.

Rani counted below her breath and then wrote something on the chart at the foot of Jessa's bed.

"How do you feel this morning?"

"Well, actually, my arm hurts."

96

"The doctor left an order for something you can have with your breakfast to help that. It's going to hurt for a while yet. Sprains often hurt a lot more than breaks, you know."

"Oh great. When can I ride again?"

"Ride?" Rani looked up from the blood-pressure cuff she was wrapping around Jessa's unbandaged arm.

"Two, three weeks—you have to check with your doctor. It's hard to say. Hmph. Ride? Your mother said you would ask that. My dear girl, how about you just concentrate on getting better! You'll ride again soon enough. What's the rush?"

"But when?" Jessa insisted. "How long. . . ."

Rani cut her off with a sharp shake of her head. She listened intently through her stethoscope and then let the air hiss out of the blood pressure cuff.

"Now, how about letting that friend of yours in to say hello?"

"Sure. Who is it?"

"I can't remember the name—sit tight and get started on your breakfast. I'll fetch them from the waiting room."

"Them?"

"She brought her father."

Jessa was trying to nudge a rubbery bit of egg onto her toast when Rachel Blumen and her father walked in. Jessa gave up on the egg and put her fork down. Life was quite a bit more difficult with only one hand.

"Hello there, kiddo!" boomed Mr. Blumen. He strode over to her bed and ruffled her hair. Jessa cringed inwardly. She hated it when people called her "kiddo." She hated it even more when people ruffled her hair.

"You're looking pretty good! I just wanted to come by and say 'Thank you' in person for saving my little girl and Gazelle."

Jessa glanced at Rachel who was staring down at the floor and blushing.

"Um . . . I didn't really do anything—I think I just got in the way, really," stammered Jessa.

"Nonsense! You and that Krystal. . . ."

"Cheryl," corrected Rachel and Jessa in unison.

"Cheryl. If you two hadn't come along when you did and then gone for help—well, I don't want to think what might have happened."

He gave Rachel's shoulder a quick squeeze. Rachel kept staring at the floor. She didn't look too happy to be there.

"You girls go ahead and have a bit of a visit. I'll be in the waiting room, kiddo," he said to Rachel.

At least I don't need to feel picked on, thought Jessa. Obviously he called everyone 'kiddo.'

After he had gone, Jessa smiled at Rachel. Suddenly the room seemed very quiet.

"You want some egg?"

Rachel shook her head.

"How is Gazelle?"

"The vet came by yesterday. She gave me some cream for the scrapes on her legs. She didn't even need stitches or anything. The vet couldn't believe it."

"I guess we were all pretty lucky."

"Except you."

"What do you mean?" asked Jessa.

"Well, not being able to go in the show is pretty bad luck."

"It's okay—there are lots more shows if we don't make it to this one."

Rachel shook her head and bit her bottom lip. She looked really upset.

"Really, Rachel—it's okay—don't worry about it. The whole thing was an accident."

"It's not that . . ." Rachel looked as if she were going to cry.

"What's the matter?"

Rachel looked as if something were choking her. Jessa could hardly hear her when she finally spoke.

"You won't believe what my dad said in the car on the way here."

"What?" Jessa wasn't sure she wanted to know. *Maybe he was going to take Gazelle away. That would be terrible for Rachel.*

"He said he was glad at least *I'd* be able to compete for his dumb trophy."

Jessa looked at Rachel. She still didn't quite understand why she was so upset. It was hardly surprising her father would be relieved his daughter wasn't hurt and could still compete.

"Then he said that you didn't have much of a chance anyway so it didn't really matter that you couldn't ride at the show."

"Oh," Jessa said slowly. "Well, maybe he was just

joking. You know, trying to make you feel better."

Rachel shook her head. "I got really mad and I told him I was going to withdraw and then we had this big argument and he started yelling that if I didn't want a show horse I should just say so."

Rachel folded her arms across her chest. Jessa could see she was struggling not to cry.

"You're so lucky. I bet your mom doesn't say stuff like that," Rachel said, staring at the floor. Jessa had no idea what to say. If she agreed, it would just make Rachel feel worse.

Rachel looked up and saw Jessa watching her.

Her voice was harder when she spoke again. "Hey, just forget it. We argue like that all the time. It doesn't mean anything."

Finally Jessa spoke.

"Look, it's okay. Go in the show. There's no reason not to. I'll be watching even if I can't ride."

Rachel sighed. "I'm sorry about what happened on the bridge. I was so dumb to try and lead her across—I didn't think she would fall through—I thought it would be strong enough. . . . And I'm sorry about all the things I said about you and Jeremy and I'm sorry I gave him a wrong number when he asked for yours. . . ."

"You did what?" Jessa laughed in spite of herself. Rachel was clearly not having a good day and if she had to drive home with that sour-puss father of hers, it obviously wasn't going to get any better.

"Am I interrupting anything?"

Jessa and Rachel both looked towards the room door to see who had spoken. Jeremy smiled at both of them. He sat on the edge of Jessa's bed and presented her with a large bunch of flowers and a horse novel.

"For the Rain Rider," the card said.

"Oh, thank you, Jeremy. They're beautiful!" gasped Jessa.

"I hope you're not in here long enough to read the whole book," he said. "How are you going to get ready for the Spring Classic if you're lying around in bed?"

"I guess I'm not," Jessa said, looking at Rachel.

Rachel didn't look up. She was studying the folded blanket on the foot of Jessa's bed. She looked flushed and unhappy.

"Jeez! Is someone having a party in here without inviting me?"

Cheryl bounced into the room and hopped up onto the other side of Jessa's bed. She leaned over as if to inspect Jessa's sling and bandage and then tipped her head up so only Jessa could see her face. She wiggled her eyebrows frantically up and down and rolled her eyes in Jeremy's general direction.

Jessa laughed and pushed Cheryl away playfully with her good arm.

Just then Jessa's mother walked into the room.

"Good grief! Where did all these people come from? When I left you were sleeping! Hi Cheryl— what on earth are you doing?"

"Hi, Mrs. Richardson. I was just inspecting the

medical handiwork here."

Jessa and Cheryl laughed again.

Jessa's mother handed her a parcel. "This was left at the nurse's station for you."

Jessa took the package. With Cheryl's help she tore off the wrapping paper. Inside was a pair of brand new jodhpurs.

She held them up with her good hand.

"Look, Mom! Jods! Who are they from?"

Cheryl opened the card and read the message.

"Hope to see you back in the saddle soon!
Best wishes from the ladies at Dark Creek Stables."

The card was signed by Mrs. Bailey, Sharon Davies, Marjorie Hamilton and Betty King—all the women who kept their horses at Dark Creek Stables.

Jessa beamed at everyone in the room.

"I can't wait to try them out," she said.

"It's lucky you all came to visit so early," Jessa's mother said. "I just met Jessa's doctor in the hall and he said she could go home as soon as she has finished her breakfast."

Jessa grinned. As far as she was concerned, she'd been lying around quite long enough. She was feeling much better already.

Chapter Ten

"Why do you think Rachel's dad is so mean?" Jessa asked her mother as they drove home from the hospital.

Jessa's mother stared at the road ahead. She didn't answer right away.

"I've only met him a couple of times—at school functions. He seemed a bit loud to me. But I don't know about mean."

"He seems really grumpy to me, like he's mad all the time."

"Nobody can be mad all the time, thank goodness. I don't know, Jessa. I would say it's less likely that he is truly 'mean' and more likely that he's someone who just doesn't consider other people's feelings before he speaks."

Jessa looked down at her sling and thought of the trophy Mr. Blumen had donated to the horse show, the trophy Rachel would probably win. She sighed. She was glad she wasn't Rachel, trophy or no trophy.

By the time they arrived home, there were several

messages on the answering machine. There were three from Cheryl and one from Mrs. Bailey.

Jessa phoned Mrs. Bailey right away.

"Thank you so much for the jods," she said. "They fit perfectly!"

"You're welcome, dear. Now, you hurry up and get well so you can get back to work."

Jessa swallowed hard. She hadn't thought about what would happen to the stalls while she was recuperating.

"Who's going to muck out?" she asked.

"Don't you worry about a thing. Marjorie will help during the week and Sharon and Betty will take turns on the weekends. We have it all under control."

"Should I come down and help feed?" Jessa offered, ignoring her mother's hand signals which Jessa assumed to mean "STAY AWAY FROM THE BARN!"

"Nonsense," Mrs. Bailey snorted at the other end of the line. "We managed before. I guess we can muddle through until you're back on your feet. I'll keep a special eye on that pony of yours."

"Thank you, Mrs. Bailey. I'll be back as soon as I can."

"I'm sure you will, dear."

Cheryl's messages were not quite as easy to decipher. Each one sounded stranger than the one before.

"I have a horse-less plan for the one-armed horsewoman. We must meet immediately!" *Beeeeep.* . . .

Jessa pushed the "play" button to listen to the next message.

"Be prepared for a test of four-legged wood-riding ability." *Beeeeep.* . . .

Jessa's eyebrows scrunched together when she heard that. For a minute she forgot how much her arm hurt. The last message made no sense at all.

"Await the mighty Madame C and her trusty steed, Vidal Sassoon!" *Beeeeep.* . . .

"*What* is that girl plotting now?" asked Jessa's mother. "You sure have some interesting friends."

"Can she come over?"

"Of course. I can't wait to meet this steed of hers. But I'm warning you, don't even ask if you can go to the barn."

Jessa sighed. In truth, her arm ached so much she didn't feel like going anyway.

Jessa was lying in her bed when she heard someone clumping up the stairs.

"Cheryl?"

A booming voice answered.

"No! It is I, Madame C, with my trusty, hairy stallion, Vidal! Open the royal stable door so that we may enter!"

Carefully, Jessa got off the bed. She seemed to be getting stiffer, not better. She opened the door and saw Cheryl brandishing a two-by-four piece of wood about one metre long.

Dozens of coloured ribbons hung from nails fastened to one end.

"What is that?" asked Jessa.

Cheryl swooped regally past her, the ribbons fluttering and trailing behind.

"Vidal," declared Cheryl, "the One-Armed Horsewoman's training equipment."

Cheryl eased her heavy backpack down onto the bed. She put the two-by-four beside it, sat down and opened her pack.

"I went to the library." She pulled out several books and read the title of the first one.

"*Horsemanship* by Waldemar Seunig. He's German—it must be good."

"What are we going to do with all these books?"

"As your official coach, I have designed a specialized training program for you." Cheryl opened another book and scanned the page. "How many beats are in the trot?"

"Four."

"Excellent! We'll have you winning that Classic in no time."

Jessa eased herself down on the bed beside Cheryl. "I really don't think it's going to happen," she said.

Cheryl looked at her. "Have faith, my child," she said dramatically. "That is why we shall practice here in the royal stable yard." She reached inside the backpack and pulled out Rebel's bridle.

"What's *that* for?" Jessa asked, totally confused.

"Sitzen on zee flat-backed four-legged pony," Cheryl commanded and pulled Jessa's wooden chair out from under her writing desk.

Jessa did as she was told and straddled the chair backwards. She watched as Cheryl looped the head-piece over her head like a giant necklace. Cheryl took the bit in her hands and stepped between the reins.

"Picken-zee up zee reins from zee floor-en-zee."

Jessa reached forward with her good arm and picked up the reins. She looped them over the back of the chair.

"This is kind of silly. I can't even hold the reins with my other hand."

"Vee shall use zee one-armed method! Sitzen-zee up-en-zee."

Jessa humoured her friend and sat up as straight as she could on her chair-sized pony. Despite herself, she clucked encouragement to her odd-looking mount. Madame C picked up a brisk trot in place and jiggled the bit up and down. Jessa held both reins with her good hand. Almost by instinct she found herself adjusting them until they were even. She even managed to keep light contact with the bit which wasn't easy given all the bouncing around her friend was doing.

Madame C snorted and tossed her head. She leaned forward and read from "*Horsemanship*" which was propped up on the dresser in front of her.

"Allow me to read from the chapter on riding manners." Cheryl cleared her voice dramatically.

"First of all, there is one's behaviour towards older riders and the fair sex, which lends true charm to our riding pleasures in the hunting field. . . ."

"The fair sex?" Jessa giggled.

"Not everyone is as firm in the saddle as you are," continued Cheryl seriously, "and when you rapidly pass an older gentleman who comfortably jogs along for the sake of his health, or a young lady on a thoroughbred that recalls its youth on the turf only too often, you will not make many friends."

Jessa whooped with laughter. "You're making this up!"

"No, really, read it yourself—this chapter will be your homework so you know how to behave properly next time you meet Jeremy on the trail. Can you imagine! That's how they used to talk fifty years ago when this book came out."

"Whoa, Nellie!" Jessa said and pulled back on the reins. Her horse took the bridle from her and hung it from the bedroom doorknob.

"Enough of that," said Cheryl. "Let's move now to the grooming lesson."

"Grooming?"

"Braiding to be exact. With Vidal here."

Cheryl took her two-by-four and leaned it against the dresser. "We can practice braiding tails with all these coloured ribbons. Well, I can practice braiding. You read the instructions to me from that book on showing."

Jessa moved slowly to the bed and sorted through books on everything from cross country jump building to grooming, equitation, training, and barrel racing. She certainly had enough to read while she was recuperating.

"These must have weighed at ton! Oh, here it is."

She flipped through a book on preparing for horse shows until she found the section on tail braiding.

"Okay—it says the hairs should be as long and even as possible."

"Fear not, my friend. I pre-pulled Vidal's mane and tail. For convenience and ease of handling, I only brought along his tail."

Jessa kept reading. "You're supposed to make the hair damp. . . . Look at these pictures—this looks very complicated."

"Just pretend the hairs are wet already."

"Okay, okay. Take a small strand from each side of the dock. . . ."

Cheryl picked up two ribbons from each side at the top of the two-by-four.

"Now take a third piece from one side, and a fourth from the other and braid down the middle taking in pieces from the sides."

"What?" Cheryl twisted four groups of ribbons together.

"That doesn't look right. Here—look at the picture," Jessa said.

"That doesn't look like what you were reading."

"Okay. Start again. Take one piece . . . no, I mean two pieces from either side. . . . Be careful you don't get kicked!"

Cheryl grinned. "It's a good thing we're practicing this now instead of the morning of the show."

Jessa looked at the knotted mass of ribbons her friend held out to her and nodded in agreement. But inside, she didn't think it mattered. She couldn't see how she, or Rebel, or her trusty groom, Madame C, could possibly be ready for the Arbutus Lane Spring Horse Show.

Chapter Eleven

Jessa turned off the alarm clock early the next morning. She dozed lightly, trying not to think about the prospect of going back to school. Half-asleep, she heard the phone ring downstairs. Her bedroom door was open and she could just make out her mother's voice. *Who could be calling so early?*

"Actually, I think she is still asleep. May I ask who's calling? . . . Jeremy . . . does she have your number?"

Jeremy! Jessa swung her legs stiffly over the side of the bed. *I guess this is what it feels like to be really old*, she thought as she hobbled across the room. *Poor Mrs. Bailey.*

"Mom!" she yelled. "I'm up! I'm coming down."

"Just a minute—I think I hear her on the stairs."

A moment later Jessa took the receiver from her mother.

"Hello?"

"Hi, Jessa. How are you feeling? Did I wake you up?"

"No. No—I was just about to get up to get ready for school. I'm feeling a bit better. Really sore."

"I guess that's to be expected. I'm sorry to call so

early. My mom's on her way out to the Blumen's and I wanted to talk to you before she leaves. Are you still interested in going to the Spring Classic in those first year horse and rider hunter classes?"

"Well . . . yes, but I don't think I can. . . ."

Jeremy didn't stop to listen to her protest.

"I thought of a way to keep Rebel fit while you get better."

"How?"

"I could ride him for you."

"You could?"

"Sure. That way he'll stay in good shape. You can watch and see what I do with him. But I saw how you ride. You'll be fine even if you only get to ride him a day or two before the show."

"Oh, Jeremy—I don't know what to say . . . I. . . ."

"Great. Can you talk to Cheryl today? She could take Rebel over to the Blumen's—it's not that far from Dark Creek—and then your Mom can drive you over there to meet us. She already said she'd do the driving."

"She did?"

"Sure, why wouldn't she?" Jeremy didn't wait for Jessa to say anything else. "The Blumens have a good training ring. Everything should be fine. The only thing left to do is for my mom to ask Mr. Blumen if it's okay."

"Mr. Blumen?" Jessa still wasn't convinced the plan would work.

"Don't worry. He thinks you're great for saving Rachel."

"But . . ." Jessa thought of what Rachel had told her at the hospital.

"Look, all you need to say is 'yes'. Leave all the planning to me. Well?"

"Well . . . okay—yes, I guess! Thank you!"

"No problem. I'll get my mom to arrange for the first training session tomorrow after school."

"Wow . . ." Cheryl said with awe that day at lunch. "What a nice thing to do. I think I should stick around for the training session, too—don't you? I mean, as your official coach I don't think I should miss this, do you?"

Jessa interrupted her friend who was so excited she nearly knocked over her bowl of chicken noodle soup.

"You'll be there—you have to ride Rebel over from Dark Creek," Jessa reminded her.

"No problem. No problem. Rebel's a good boy. We'll be fine—don't worry."

Cheryl slurped her noodle soup loudly. "Did you know they slurp noodles like this in Japan?"

"Yes, actually, I did know that. My dad lives there, remember?"

"Oh, yeah—right." Cheryl slurped loudly again and Jessa watched a pale strand of noodle slither into her friend's mouth. "Is it true that the louder you slurp, the more you like the food?"

"Something like that. But I do believe that here in Canada slurping your noodles is rude. Disgusting actually."

Cheryl grinned and picked up the bowl. She

drained it in two gulps, slurping noisily.

Jessa looked around to see if anyone else had noticed. The cafeteria was full of kids having lunch. Luckily the noise level was pretty high and only some fourth grade boys were sitting at the next table. Even when they were trying to have good manners they sounded at least as bad as Cheryl.

"Have you picked your poet yet?" Cheryl asked.

"Yuck," said Jessa. She didn't like poetry. It didn't make any sense to her. She hadn't even started to look for a poem to memorize. She dreaded having to get up in front of the whole class to recite one. Even worse, their English teacher, Mr. Wiggens, wanted the class to find Canadian poets because they were doing a unit on Canadian literature.

Jessa decided that at least in one way she took after her mother—they both liked numbers. She could understand why her mother liked the order and neatness of her giant ledger sheets, all the numbers lined up perfectly and adding up. Numbers made sense to her—poetry did not.

"I found this great book on my brother's bookshelf," Cheryl said, licking her fingers.

Cheryl's older brother was really weird. He went to the University of Victoria and studied theatre or Greek or something. He wore a long black coat everywhere and a bright red scarf—even in the summer. Jessa thought he was a bit creepy but Cheryl insisted he was just working at being eccentric.

Jessa looked at the book Cheryl pulled out of her

bag. It had a yellow cover and a photograph of a chair on the front. "Hey—just like the flat-backed pony!" Cheryl took the book back from her and flipped through it.

"There's a really cool poem in here that's kind of like a story."

"Yeah?" Jessa poked at her leftover salad. She didn't think there was such a thing as a 'cool poem'.

"It's about this woman who dressed up like a man so she could be a soldier in the civil war. She was a spy!"

"What kind of a stupid story is that? No woman would want to be a soldier."

"Well, for your information, this happens to be a true story. It was some old relative of the author's. And the author . . . this Sandy Shreve person . . . happens to live in Vancouver. So there. A Canadian woman poet who wrote about a spy who was a woman dressed up like a man who pretended to be a woman. . . ."

"What??? That doesn't make any sense."

"When she was in the army she was a spy and she had to dress up in all these different costumes. Once she even dressed up as an old peddler woman—even though all the other soldiers thought she was a man."

"Oh, come on. I don't believe you."

"Read it yourself! It's right here in the book. I'm going to dress up like an old peddler woman and recite the poem about her spying. Will you help me memorize it?"

Jessa shrugged. "I guess so. Will you help me find

a poem to learn?"

"Sure. My brother has lots of books. "

"Nothing too strange, okay? And nothing too long."

"Okay, okay. Now, listen." Cheryl hunched over, took off her glasses and scrunched up her face.

"What are you doing?" Jessa asked.

"I'm acting like an old woman who is too poor to buy eyeglasses . . . were glasses even invented back then?"

Jessa shrugged. "I don't even know when the Civil War happened. What were they fighting about, anyway?"

Cheryl talked in a croaky old woman's voice. "According to the book Franklin went to war in 1861."

"Who's Franklin?"

"That's my name . . . the name I took when I pretended to be a man. We went to war to join God's fight to end slavery."

Jessa had to admit her friend was pretty convincing. She sounded as if she was a hundred years old. Trust Cheryl to find the one interesting poem on the planet.

> *"Yet Emma's triumph must have been*
> *when Franklin crossed the Chickahominy*
> *dressed as an old Irish peddler*
> *selling her poor wares on the other side of the line*
> *a mustard plaster to blister her face*
> *pepper to redden her eyes*

A woman masquerading as a man
impersonates a woman
No one begins to guess
that this young lad they love to tease . . ."

Cheryl stopped. "I can't remember how it goes after that."

"How did she get away with it?" asked Jessa. "How could nobody notice? I mean women have . . . you know . . . well, breasts!"

"I guess she bandaged them so they didn't stick out so much."

"Ooooh! That must have hurt! Why would anyone want to be a soldier that badly?"

"Well what if only boys were allowed to ride horses and that's what you really wanted to do? Wouldn't you cut off your hair and wear baggy clothes so you could?"

Jessa leaned back on her chair. She wasn't sure if she would want to go through all that trouble, even for riding. Besides, riding was fun and going to war wasn't.

"Don't look now—there's a teacher heading right for our table!"

Jessa turned around and immediately wished she hadn't. Miss Woolf, the music teacher at Kenwood Elementary, was heading straight towards her. Jessa couldn't help feeling guilty even though she had no idea what she had done wrong.

Miss Woolf handed her an envelope.

"This was left for you at the office," she said. "I'm on lunch supervision today so I said I'd try to find you."

117

"Oh. Thank you," Jessa said.

Jessa and Cheryl looked at each other and then at the envelope. Jessa turned it over. There was no return address on the back, either.

"Well, open it!" Cheryl said as soon as the teacher had gone.

Jessa fumbled with her good hand and finally managed to take out the note inside.

Dear Rain Rider,
Everything is organized for tomorrow. Please have Rebel at the Blumen's training ring at 5:30 PM. Your mother will drop you off if Cheryl can ride Rebel over. See you then,
J.D.

"J. D.? Jeremy Digsby?" Cheryl sighed. "A hand-written, hand-delivered note! That is just *so* romantic."

"Oh, stop!" said Jessa, poking her friend in the ribs. "You will ride Rebel over there for me, won't you?"

"Maybe," teased Cheryl. "If I have time. . . ." The girls laughed.

"Hey, since Rebel's not going anywhere tonight, do you want to come to my house after school? I could help you find a poem," Cheryl offered.

"Sure, I guess so." Jessa thought she would rather be doing almost anything else other than looking through poetry books, but if she didn't bite the bullet and get started on the project, she was going to get a zero on her assignment.

Chapter Twelve

Jeremy swung easily into the saddle and picked up Rebel's reins. Jessa and Cheryl sat on a low jump in the middle of the Blumen's training ring and watched.

"He's so good," whispered Cheryl.

"I know. He's so smooth to ride," agreed Jessa.

"Not Rebel! I'm talking about Jeremy!"

Both girls giggled as they watched Jeremy put Rebel through his paces. He rode so easily and with such confidence it seemed Rebel knew what he was supposed to do almost before Jeremy asked.

After about fifteen minutes of warming up, Jeremy rode over to Jessa and Cheryl.

"How's the arm?" he asked, looking down at them.

"It's okay—a little better, I guess."

Cheryl piped up. "Better? You should have seen her riding on the weekend. . . ." Cheryl let out a little yelp when Jessa kicked her. Jessa couldn't imagine anything worse than Jeremy knowing she had spent her Sunday afternoon riding a chair.

"Reading," Jessa hastily added. "I was reading—a training book from Germany."

Jeremy smiled. "That's the spirit! Just like a true Rain Rider!"

Cheryl nudged Jessa in the ribs. Jessa poked her back. Sometimes Cheryl was such a pain.

"I'm going to ride Caspian right after Rebel. We'll have them both in great shape for the show! Don't worry about a thing."

"Yeah. Don't worry," Cheryl echoed as Jeremy rode away from them. "You and Rebel are going to be great."

Jessa wished she shared her friend's optimism. She didn't say anything, though. She was too busy admiring the way Jeremy rode her horse. Rebel looked so relaxed. Every now and then one of his ears would flick back to listen to Jeremy.

"Now what are they doing?" asked Cheryl.

Jessa watched Jeremy guiding Rebel diagonally across the arena.

"He's leg-yielding! I didn't know Rebel could do that!"

Jeremy rode past the girls again from the opposite direction. One after the other Rebel performed half-passes, turns on the forehand, as well as turns over the haunches. He backed straight and then collected and extended smoothly and easily at all three gaits.

Jeremy picked up the canter from a walk and he and Rebel performed a perfect flying change just as they crossed in front of the girls.

Jeremy halted from the canter and gave Rebel a warm pat on the neck. Rebel looked positively pleased with himself.

"Somewhere along the way this old guy had some good training. He really knows his stuff." Jeremy sounded genuinely impressed.

Jessa beamed. She had never doubted Rebel's abilities. But she also knew she had a lot to learn before she could ride him as well as Jeremy.

Jeremy turned Rebel away and rode for a little longer on the flat. Then he took a couple of small cross-poles before he let Rebel walk around the ring on a loose rein.

"Can you get the gate for me, Cheryl? I'm just going to take him down the driveway and back to cool him out a bit. I'll be back in a few minutes."

The two girls sat on the jump and chatted while they waited.

"So, what are you going to do about your poem?" asked Cheryl.

Jessa groaned and picked at a piece of thread which was hanging from her sling.

"Don't pull on that or your arm will fall off," joked Cheryl.

"I don't know what to do. I can't believe there wasn't a single, decent poem in all those books of your brother's. I told you—you found the only good one."

"Hey! I just had an idea!" said Cheryl "Mr. Wiggens never said we each had to pick a different poet. Why don't you choose another one of those Emma . . . or maybe I should say, Franklin, poems? You could do that one about how she walks through the battlefields and cuts locks of hair off the corpses."

"That was disgusting!"

"She did it for a good reason," argued Cheryl. "Think how happy their mothers and sweethearts would have been to get something like that in the mail."

"I think that's even more disgusting."

"Well, I think it's romantic. Almost as romantic as Jeremy riding your wonder horse to get him in shape for the show."

Jessa blushed.

"Oooooh! You're blushing!"

"Get lost! I am not."

No doubt about it, Cheryl was at her annoying best. But Jessa had to admit her idea about memorizing one of the Emma poems was a pretty good one. She'd start that night right after supper.

Jessa sat straight up in bed in the middle of the night. Her heart pounded and her eyes strained to see through the darkness.

In her dream she had been riding Rebel across a battlefield. She didn't want to look down to see the dead men. Rebel kept jumping over them but Jessa could only hold onto his mane with one hand.

In the distance Jessa could see Rachel and Jeremy holding hands. She tried to make Rebel gallop faster. Then she felt a hand reach up from below to grab her ankle and try to pull her off her horse.

That was when she woke up. Her blankets were twisted around her feet. No wonder it had seemed so real.

She straightened the bedclothes and tried to go back to sleep.

"What it takes to keep trudging through the muck
the unstoppable rain sucking her feet
deep and deeper as if each next step
would be her grave . . ."

The lines of the poem about Franklin Thompson, Field Nurse of the Potomac—alias Emma—repeated themselves over and over again in Jessa's head. Maybe Shakespeare would have been safer.

She fell asleep trying to remember how the next verse went but the only lines which would come to her were,

"Emma is unstoppable
gallops straight into the fray again and again with
mercy . . ."

On Saturday morning Jessa heard her mother at the door of her bedroom.

"Jessa?" Her mother knocked gently again. "Jessa? Are you awake?"

"I am now," Jessa grumbled.

Her mother came in and sat on the wooden chair at Jessa's desk.

"I don't know how you manage, but it looks as if you're going to get out of watching Bucky again today."

"How?" Jessa's head still wasn't quite clear of sleep. She sat up in bed.

"I just talked to Jeremy's mother on the phone. She called to ask if you could come to the Blumen's at one o'clock. She offered to give you a riding lesson."

"But—I still can't use my wrist."

"That's what I told her. She said it didn't matter. She is going to use a . . . a . . . I think she said a plumb line."

"A plumb line? Are you sure?"

"I don't know. She said there was some way you could ride and you wouldn't have to steer because she would be holding the plumb line."

"Oh! I know—a lunge line!"

"Right! That's it. Anyway, she said it would be perfectly safe and her son is insisting you need to ride."

Jessa planned to meet Cheryl at Dark Creek Stables at noon. It sure felt good to be back at the barn, and wearing her new jods, after a whole week of just watching.

"Hi, Jessa. How are you feeling?" Marjorie Hamilton asked.

She was just finishing going over her Morgan mare, Babe, with a soft brush.

"Better, thanks," Jessa said. "I'm riding for the first time today since the accident."

"Getting ready for the horse show?"

"Maybe," Jessa said. "I'll see how it goes." She was impressed with how unconcerned she sounded.

"Well, if you do make it, we'll be competing

against each other next weekend."

"We will?" asked Jessa.

"Babe and I are still in our first year together. I bought her at the end of last summer."

"You can jump?" Jessa asked, hoping she didn't sound too rude.

"It's only a little course. I'm taking Babe down to the Equestrian Centre today to let her have a good look at the place before the show."

"Good luck," Jessa offered, running her hand along the sturdy mare's neck. With the exception of her white blaze and two white socks, Babe was the colour of pale milk chocolate.

"I'm sure you'll do fine," Jessa added generously. She hoped Marjorie wasn't going to have hot flushes or a heart attack or anything with all the excitement of the big horse show.

Just then Cheryl arrived on her bike. Very confidently, she caught Rebel and led him out of his paddock. She let him munch some grass along the driveway until Marjorie and Babe were finished in the cross-ties.

As Cheryl briskly worked on Rebel, whisking the stiff body brush over his back, under his belly and across his haunches, Jessa noticed just how good her friend was getting at grooming her horse.

All week she had been taking him over to the Blumen's for Jeremy's schooling sessions, and it showed.

Jessa stood at Rebel's head and rubbed behind his ears while Cheryl adjusted the saddle.

"You were great yesterday," Cheryl said to Jessa as she tightened Rebel's girth. He puffed himself up and Jessa gave him a piece of carrot to distract him. Cheryl took advantage of the moment and tightened the girth another hole.

"Not as good as you," Jessa replied. "That old shawl was perfect. And your makeup was excellent—those looked like real wrinkles."

"Well, I think that was a stroke of genius when you decided to recite that poem from flat on your back on the floor."

"I thought I looked like a wounded soldier with my sling. It was easier than trying to figure out cute little actions for every word like Rachel did with her sweet garden poem."

"I'll bet you never thought you'd get an 'A' on a poetry assignment," said Cheryl.

"Nope. You are right there," agreed Jessa.

"You know what else I'm right about?"

"What?"

"You are going to win at the Spring Classic next weekend."

Jessa didn't answer. She watched Cheryl mount up and turn Rebel down the driveway. She got into her mother's car for the short drive over to the Blumen Estate. She didn't know who would be more disappointed if she couldn't ride next weekend.

Getting mounted was just the first challenge of Jessa's lesson with Jeremy's mother. In the end, she had to climb up on the top rail of the fence with one hand and Cheryl's help. Then Jeremy maneuvered Rebel into position beside her.

Holding onto Rebel's mane with her right hand she carefully stretched her leg over his back and then settled gently down into the saddle. When her feet found the stirrups she sat up straight and smiled. She was on her horse again. From up there, anything seemed possible.

Things went quite smoothly in the first part of the lesson.

Jessa did fine as long as Rebel didn't go faster than a walk. Rebecca told her what to do with a steady stream of instructions. After just a few minutes it was clear why Jeremy was such a good rider. Right from the start, Jessa had to ride without any reins.

"You have to ride off your leg—remember, you can do this even when you have your reins back. Ask him to move to the outside of the circle by using your inside leg . . . that's it."

Jessa felt Rebel move away from the pressure of her leg. Soon they were making a large circle around Rebecca who watched them carefully and held the other end of the lunge line.

"Look up! Stretch your legs long. Longer! Better . . . good. Now—ask him to halt."

Jessa looked at Rebecca blankly. Had she forgotten that she had just recently tied Rebel's reins in a knot so Jessa couldn't use them?

"Tighten the muscles in your back, sit down into the saddle—resist his forward movement. . . ."

Jessa did the best she could and was surprised to feel Rebel slow down and then stop obediently.

"Now, an even squeeze with your legs and ask him to move forward again. . . ."

Jessa did as she was told and Rebel stepped out into a relaxed walk.

"That's amazing," she said.

"Jeremy is right about that horse of yours. He's had some great schooling," answered Rebecca.

When Rebecca told her to ask for a trot, Jessa felt her confidence evaporate. *How could she possibly ride well without reins? Doing the exercises at a walk was one thing, but trotting?*

Jessa squeezed her lower legs and Rebel picked up the trot. Jessa bounced around so much she felt as if she had never been on a horse before! As she came around the circle, she saw her mother and Cheryl standing at the fence together. *What a day for her mother to stay and watch her ride!*

"Keep your head up! Keep your weight down in your heels. Relax! Stretch up tall. Sit deeper into the saddle. Use your rhythm to slow him down!"

Jessa tried hard to do what Rebecca told her. She held her sprained wrist close to her stomach with her good hand so it didn't get jarred too badly. Even so, it hurt every time she bumped down on the saddle.

"Sit up straight!"

Her whole body felt stiff and uncooperative as Rebel trotted around and around.

"There! How does that feel?"

"Te-e-e-rrible," Jessa answered, her voice bouncing along with the rest of her.

"Well it looks a bit better. Pick up your rising trot . . . there, good—watch your diagonal. . . ."

Soon Jessa's back hurt, her legs ached and her wrist throbbed whenever she jerked it suddenly to keep her balance.

"That's better! Keep those heels down!"

Jessa didn't think any riding lesson had ever taken so long to finally come to an end.

"Don't give up," Rebecca said, patting Rebel on the shoulder. "That's always hard the first time you you ride without reins. You're lucky, Jessa. You have a good partner here. He'll look after you. Now, you look after him and ride to the end of the drive and back to cool him out. You walk along, too, Cheryl, in case they have a problem."

"Okay." Jessa studied her muddy riding boots. "Thanks for all your help." She was so tired and stiff she didn't even think to feel insulted that her friend was being sent along to walk beside her.

By the time Jessa, Cheryl and Rebel got back, Jessa could see Rebecca and her mother talking at the gate to the training ring. Her mother smiled as Jessa rode up to the two women.

"Thanks again for your help," Jessa said, getting ready to dismount.

"I'm not finished with you yet."

Jessa looked down at Jeremy's mother in surprise.

"I want to see you back here tomorrow at the same time—and on Monday after school. The show's exactly one week away. You can give him Friday night off when you clean your tack. Otherwise, I expect you to be here every afternoon right after school."

Jessa looked at her mother. She knew they couldn't afford private lessons every day. Not even for a week.

"It's okay, Jessa," her mother said. "Don't look so shocked. Guess who needs help doing her taxes?"

"Really?" Jessa said. "I can have a lesson every day until the show?"

Her mother nodded. She looked extremely pleased with herself.

Jessa looked back at the tall, slender horse trainer. She had the same kind, determined eyes as her son. "You don't seriously think I'll be ready, do you?" Jessa asked.

Rebecca met Jessa's gaze steadily.

"Yes, Jessa. I seriously do. Will I see you tomorrow?"

Jessa nodded silently. *Oh great*, she thought. *Someone else to disappoint.*

When Jessa finally dismounted with Rebecca's help, her knees nearly buckled under her weight. Her legs felt like jelly as she staggered back a couple of steps.

Cheryl took Rebel's reins and got ready to mount up for the ride back to the barn. She didn't say anything and neither did Jessa. Her friend's silence wasn't a good sign. Cheryl always had something to say. Jessa knew her well enough to know what she was thinking, though. It was the same thing Jessa was thinking.

Even with lessons every day, she was going to make a fool of herself at the Arbutus Lane show.

"How's your wrist?" Cheryl asked.

Jessa stopped oiling her stirrup leather and turned her wrist slowly from side to side.

"It's okay if I don't try to turn it too far." Jessa slowly turned her wrist to the left and then back again. "I still can't lift anything. I might be able to hold the reins but if he does anything wrong I won't be able to steer."

Jessa's room looked like a very messy tack shop. Her saddle was draped over the back of the wooden chair, the girth, and a spare one she had borrowed from Mrs. Bailey, lay on newspaper on top of the dresser. Cheryl was surrounded by bits and pieces of the bridle which she had spread out all over the floor.

"I sure hope you can put that back together right," Jessa said.

"Don't worry. I have this diagram right here. So, are you nervous?" Cheryl asked.

"About the bridle or about the show?"

"The show, of course."

Jessa shrugged. "Kind of. In a way, I've given up already."

"As your coach, I say that's a dumb way to talk. You're supposed to imagine yourself doing everything perfectly. All the Olympic riders do that."

Jessa closed her eyes and pictured herself asking Rebel for a smooth transition from canter to trot using only her legs and back. In her mind's eye she bounced hard in the saddle the same way she'd been doing on the lunge line most of the week.

"I don't think it will work," she said.

"It certainly won't if you don't believe in the technique. It's called positive visualization. My brother has a book on it."

"Look, I'll be quite happy if I don't fall off," said Jessa. "Let's hurry up and finish this tack. We have to get up at five o'clock—remember?"

Cheryl groaned. "How could I forget?"

Jessa and Cheryl were at Dark Creek by 5:30 the next morning.

"You don't look so good, Mrs. Richardson," Cheryl said.

Jessa's mother moaned and took another sip out of her Starbuck's coffee mug.

"Here, Jessa," she said, pressing some money into her daughter's hand. Your entry fees. You can pay me back out of your baby-sitting money, if you ever get around to baby-sitting again."

"Thanks, Mom," Jessa said and gave her mother a quick kiss on the cheek.

"Now, if you don't need me for anything, I think I'll put the seat back and sleep in the car until the horse trailer gets here."

"Good morning, girls!" Marjorie called from over Babe's stall door. "You can have the cross-ties. I've got Babe tied in here."

She disappeared back into the stall. Jessa could hear her humming away as she worked.

Babe and Rebel were sharing a trailer ride over to the Equestrian Centre. Marjorie had arranged everything with her friend, Suzanna Tucker who owned the Oh Suzanna Tack and Feed Emporium. Jessa was glad she didn't have to ride all the way over to Arbutus Lane.

Time was tight enough without having to worry about an hour-long trail ride as well as everything else.

The girls had given Rebel a bath the day before and had braided his mane. But during the night he had rubbed some of the braids out and his tail still needed to be done.

Under the big barn lights, the girls worked quickly and quietly. Cheryl used her new braiding skills on his tail while Jessa gave him a thorough grooming.

Cheryl was just putting a little black ribbon in Rebel's braided tail when Marjorie let herself out of Babe's stall. She put her hands in the pockets of her baggy, faded overalls and inspected Cheryl's braiding job.

"A black ribbon? He's not going to a funeral. Do you mind if I have a go at this?"

Cheryl stepped back and let Marjorie move in. Her fingers moved deftly as first she undid Cheryl's work and then began to re-braid Rebel's tail. Effortlessly, she pulled in long strands of hair from either side of the dock. As the girls looked on, the braid formed perfectly. Before long it lay flat and smooth, a beautiful finish to Rebel's showy look.

"Thanks!" said Cheryl. "Can you show me how to do that?" she asked.

"Sure. But not now," Marjorie nodded. "Suzanna will be here any minute."

As the sun crept over the horizon, the horse trailer arrived. Suzanna hopped out of her pickup truck to help load the horses.

Marjorie led Babe out of her stall. The mare looked fantastic. She stepped high as if trying to lift her legs right out of her shipping bandages. An even row of neat little braids accentuated the graceful curve of her strong neck.

"Oh, she's beautiful," said Jessa as she watched the mare load into the trailer.

"Okay, girls. Your turn. Are you ready?" asked Suzanna when Babe was tied up and happily munching on some hay in the trailer.

"Ready enough," answered Cheryl.

Jessa checked Rebel's shipping bandages one last time and made sure his blanket was fastened securely. Suzanna took his lead shank from her and led Rebel up the ramp. He paused for a moment at the door to the trailer and had a good look inside. Babe nickered to him softly and Rebel decided it was safe to join her inside.

Jessa and Cheryl watched him disappear into the trailer. Suzanna and Marjorie lifted the ramp and closed the doors behind the horses.

A few minutes later, when the truck and trailer pulled away slowly, Jessa and Cheryl were busily loading gear into the back of the Richardson's old car. They packed all the grooming equipment, Rebel's tack, a water bucket, Jessa's show clothes and some carrots.

"Are you sure this show isn't lasting a week?" Jessa's mother asked, eyeing the growing mountain of stuff the girls were jamming into the hatch.

When the two girls finally settled into the back seat, Jessa was already tired.

So, this was it. Show day had finally arrived. Jessa just wished the butterflies in her stomach weren't quite so big.

Chapter Thirteen

"Remember, treat this first class like a warm-up," said Jeremy as Jessa made her way to the warm-up ring. He was leading Caspian along beside her. Caspian's black coat shone as he pranced lightly beside his owner.

"Relax, keep it slow. Use your back, your legs— remember—this is a hunter class. I have to go in a minute, and get ready for my classes. You'll be fine. Have fun!"

Jessa was so nervous she could hardly hear what Jeremy was saying. Rebel danced sideways a couple of steps when a candy wrapper fluttered in the breeze.

"Relax! You're making him nervous. He can feel how tense you are."

How could she relax? Jessa took a deep breath. Jeremy opened the gate to the warm-up ring for her and then moved out of the way with Caspian.

"You'll be fine," he repeated. "Good luck!"

Suddenly, Jessa was on her own. She took an-other deep breath, sat quietly in the saddle and asked Rebel to trot. He bounced forward, light and lively.

Oh, great. What a time for Rebel to turn into a champion show hack pony, she thought.

Jessa's arm was bandaged but she no longer wore the sling. She could hold her left rein but it still hurt to squeeze her fingers closed.

A big chestnut horse ridden by a stern-looking woman cantered past them and Rebel swished his tail.

"Okay, Rebel. Settle down," she said softly.

In the shady end of the warm-up ring, Marjorie and Babe were trotting in a circle. Marjorie was concentrating hard on getting a nice bend from Babe. Even though Babe's trot looked rather strong, Marjorie looked like her seat was glued into the saddle.

Jessa sighed. Everybody in the warm-up ring looked so calm, so competent. She adjusted her reins and tried to find a comfortable position for her injured hand.

A few minutes later the announcer's voice boomed, "and now, the first of three classes in the Arbutus Lane First Year Combination Hunter Classic Series. This must be the first year each horse-and-rider combination has been together. The first class is on the flat and the second includes a small jump. The final test of horse and rider will be over a short jump course. No obstacle will be higher than two feet. Riders will score points depending on their ranking in each class."

Jessa swallowed hard. *This was it. Too late now to back out,* she told herself firmly.

"The horse-and-rider combination which accumulates the highest number of total points will win a large trophy generously donated by the Blumen family, a cash prize of fifty dollars and a leather halter for the winning horse."

By the dramatic tone of the announcer's voice, the prize might have been $50,000 at an international competition. As Jessa rode into the show ring she felt as nervous as if she were entering the stadium at the Olympics.

One by one the horses filed into the show ring as the announcer explained how the classes would be judged. The first class was huge. By the time the gate closed, eighteen horses were walking on the rail.

Jessa spotted Rachel riding on the far side of the ring. Gazelle looked beautiful. The pair was turned out perfectly—even from a distance, Jessa could see that neither horse nor rider had a hair out of place.

Marjorie and Babe were a few horses ahead of Jessa and Rebel. Marjorie sat up very straight and Babe stepped along lightly, her soft coat gleaming in the sunshine. *Marjorie must have spent hours getting her horse ready,* Jessa thought. Jessa pushed her heels down and lifted her chin. The class had started and she was going to make the best of it!

Despite her best efforts to concentrate only on her riding, Jessa was suddenly keenly aware of her rubber riding boots and makeshift riding jacket. It wasn't even a real riding jacket but a black blazer which was too small for her mother. With the sleeves hemmed up it looked quite smart but Jessa thought that every spectator must secretly be laughing at her.

She pushed the thought from her mind and sat up even straighter. She forced herself to think not of her boots but of keeping her lower legs firmly on Rebel's sides. The hardest part, though, was keeping her hands relaxed. Her sore wrist ached already and she had been in the ring less than two minutes.

Once the judge started calling out instructions, the class seemed to fly past in a blur. Jessa concentrated on not bouncing when she made the downward transition from canter to trot, she used her back to slow the rhythm of Rebel's trot and through it all, tried to look as if she were enjoying herself.

No matter how hard she tried, it seemed she was always just a little off—not smooth enough in the canter, too fast at the trot, and too slow in all her transitions. She felt even worse when she caught a glimpse of Rachel and Gazelle gliding smoothly along at a perfectly balanced working trot. At some point, she lost track of where Marjorie and Babe were altogether.

By the time she joined the others in the line-up down the middle of the ring, she felt terrible.

She slumped in the saddle. *What had she been thinking to enter the class in the first place? What a waste of entry money!*

She looked straight ahead to avoid glancing at the bleachers where her mother and friends were sitting.

The judge talked softly into a hand-held radio and told the announcer the results of the first class. Jessa was hardly surprised to hear Rachel's name announced as the first place winner.

"And in second place, Roberta Wilmer on Black Forest, in third place, Marjorie Hamilton on Toyland Babe. . . ." Jessa caught Marjorie's eye as she rode forward to claim her ribbon. She smiled and gave her a thumbs up. *All that grooming had certainly paid off. Babe and Marjorie really looked wonderful.*

". . . and in sixth place, Jessa Richardson on Rebel."

Jessa couldn't believe her ears! She had actually placed in the ribbons! She could hear loud cheering as she rode forward to collect her ribbon. She held it high above her head and waved it at the stands where Cheryl was sitting with her mother. Cheryl waved back wildly. She spotted Mrs. Bailey's big cowboy hat in the stands behind them.

"You can give it to the ring steward to hold during the next class," the judge said.

"Congratulations, Jessa! Well done," Marjorie said from behind her.

Jessa turned around and smiled. "Congratulations to you, too," she said to Marjorie who was patting Babe's neck proudly.

"Good luck, you two!" said Marjorie and rode Babe across the ring to a clear spot on the rail as the judge announced the beginning of the next class.

Jessa was still in shock from the results of the first class when she picked up a working trot in the second.

As she and Rebel rode around the ring, Jessa tried to remember everything Rebecca had said during the week. *She might even have a chance at another ribbon.* She could almost hear Rebecca's voice. "Eyes up . . . relax. Keep your leg on . . . ease into the downward transition."

The other horses, the crowd, even the judge seemed to fade away as she concentrated completely on what she and Rebel were doing.

Even though the first part of the second class was on the flat, Jessa couldn't help thinking about the single jump she would soon have to deal with. She wished there had been more time to practice jumping during the week. As it was, Rebecca hadn't seemed overly concerned.

"The second class will just have one, single small jump," Rebecca had said. "Let's work on your two-point position on the lunge line."

"But what about the third class? The one over the jump course?" Jessa had pestered.

"Patience, Jessa. You'll be ready! Up into two-point!"

At first, Jessa hadn't been able to keep her balance for more than a couple of steps, even at the walk. Two-point was hard enough to hold even when she could rest her hands on Rebel's neck. But in her lessons with Rebecca, she wasn't allowed to use her hands at all. It was more like one-point, as far as she could see.

"You must find your balance without your hands . . . sink your weight into your heels . . . keep your legs on—don't let them slide back or you'll tip forward. . . ."

Now, in the crowded show ring, Jessa tried to recall every detail of Rebecca's lessons. She forced herself to think only of the class she was in and not to worry about the jump course coming up. It was true that there was only one jump, she reminded herself. It was also true that the vertical wasn't very high. But that would make it even more embarrassing if she fell off, or if Rebel refused, or. . . .

Jessa didn't have any more time to think of what might happen. Before she knew it the flat exercises were over and the judge directed the competitors to line up down the middle of the ring while each horse and rider in turn rode the jump. Each horse was first to canter a slow circle and then be brought back to a trot after clearing the jump. The class was judged on how steady and responsive the horse was throughout the short exercise.

Marjorie rode Babe into line beside Jessa.

"So far, so good," smiled Marjorie. As far as Jessa could tell, Marjorie was as relaxed as if she and Babe were out on a Sunday trail ride. Babe tossed her head and played with her bit and Marjorie slowly stroked her horse's neck.

The first several riders had no trouble with the jump. Then a girl took off too close and her horse popped up and over the obstacle awkwardly. A boy riding a very green thoroughbred had to circle twice before his wide-eyed mount would go over the jump.

When Jessa's turn came, she took a deep breath and asked Rebel to canter. They circled smoothly together, Jessa shortened her reins, eased into her two-point position and Rebel cleared the jump easily. She sat down in the saddle, braced her back slightly and he immediately slowed to a steady trot. She made another small circle, halted, then returned to the line-up.

Marjorie nodded and smiled when Jessa gave Rebel a pat on the neck.

"Rebel sure is a nice pony," she said kindly. "You two looked really good over that jump."

"Thank you," Jessa said and settled back into her saddle to watch the rest of the riders.

Rachel, too, managed a smooth effort over the little jump. Gazelle's ears pricked forward and she gave a little swish of her tail as she landed. Jessa wondered how on earth the judge would be able to keep all the riders straight, how he would be able to pick a winner. After each rider returned to the line-up the judge scribbled something on his clipboard.

When it was her turn to tackle the obstacle, Marjorie said, "Wish me luck!"

Babe and Marjorie didn't seem to need any luck. Their circle was perfectly round and Babe cantered so smoothly she looked like a rocking horse. She listened attentively to aids which were so subtle, Jessa could hardly tell Marjorie was giving them. *Wow. Marjorie really knows what she's doing,* Jessa marvelled as she watched Babe drop calmly to a trot right after landing the jump.

"In first place, Allison Raymond on Gold Digger. . . ." The announcer's voice echoed around the big outdoor arena. ". . . and in third place, Rachel Blumen and Gazelle."

The crowd clapped politely as Rachel rode forward.

"In fourth place, Marjorie Hamilton and Toyland Babe. . . ."

"Go Marjorie!" Mrs. Bailey shouted from the stands.

"Dark Creek! Dark Creek! Dark Creek!" chanted Cheryl.

"And in fifth place today, Jessa Richardson on Rebel. . . ."

Jessa's jaw dropped. *Fifth place?* She couldn't believe it! She and Rebel were in the ribbons again! She gave Rebel a huge pat on the neck and rode forward. Her cheeks ached from smiling so hard. She looked over to where her mother and Cheryl were sitting. Cheryl was jumping up and down and waving excitedly.

"Yay Jessa!" she shouted at the top of her lungs.

Jessa admired her ribbon before she handed it to the ring steward to hold.

"That's two," he smiled at her.

Yes, it was true. Two ribbons! She gave Rebel another pat. To think her poor pony had been living in a muddy field without any attention before she had found him!

There was a brief pause before the final class while the ring stewards set up the short jump course. Rachel rode over to Jessa and smiled.

"You two are doing very well," she said.

"Thanks," said Jessa. It was easy enough for Rachel to be generous with her praise with her first and her third place ribbons.

"It's too bad you haven't got any experience jumping courses," she said. "Maybe next time. Well, good luck."

Rachel turned and rode away before Jessa could answer. *At least her father would be pleased,* Jessa thought. It looked like she had a pretty good shot at winning the family trophy.

Jessa waited quietly with Rebel in the warm-up ring. She stayed far away from the gate so she wouldn't have to talk to Cheryl who was hovering nervously nearby, watching the riders prepare for the final class. It was all she could manage to stay calm without having to deal with her boisterous friend.

She thought again of the course she was about to negotiate. She sighed. It was true that the jump in the previous class hadn't been that bad. None of the jumps in the hunt course would be any worse. On the other hand, what would happen if Rebel refused? or spooked? or bucked in good spirits? So many things could go wrong. *Why hadn't there been more time to practice jumping?*

Jessa had tried to convince Rebecca that she wasn't prepared for the class over fences but Rebecca wouldn't budge.

"I've watched Jeremy jump him," Rebecca had insisted. "That little horse of yours knows what he's doing."

In the end, Rebecca had coached Jessa over a few cross-poles.

"Keep your eyes up—watch where you're going! Concentrate on your position. . . ."

Jessa's legs had ached after each lesson from holding her two-point position for so long.

Now, watching the ring stewards set up the jump course, Jessa struggled to slow her pounding heart. Rebecca's reassuring words did nothing to make the jumps look any easier. Jessa couldn't help it, she kept remembering her crash during her earlier riding lessons, and her near disaster over the fallen oak tree.

At last everything was ready. Each horse and rider in turn entered the ring and completed the jump course. Several horses tore around the course as if it were a jump-off.

Jessa knew they would lose marks for excessive speed in a hunter class like this. Two horses in a row refused jumps and a young girl on a big bay went off course.

Several other riders handled the course smoothly and easily, their horses jumping lightly over each obstacle.

Rachel and Gazelle's round started beautifully. No doubt about it, Gazelle was a lovely horse. She approached each fence with her ears pricked forward and an eager expression. As she jumped, her tail lifted high.

Jessa couldn't help but admire the lovely mare.

Just as Rachel approached the second-to-last jump, a little boy darted away from his mother and fell on his balloon. The balloon popped with a loud snap and Gazelle spooked sideways.

Jessa's breath caught as Rachel tried to save the jump. But Gazelle had drifted too far sideways to make it over and ducked out at the last minute to avoid crashing through the obstacle. Rachel's boot caught the jump standard as they swerved and knocked it over. The poles rolled in every direction. Gazelle tossed her head and ran sideways nearly crashing through another fence.

The boy's mother snatched him away from the side of the ring and carried him, crying, off in the direction of the parking lot.

Rachel's eyes were wide as she brought Gazelle back under control and tried to calm the young mare. She walked in a small circle while she waited for the ring stewards to set the jump up again.

Poor Rachel!, Jessa thought. *What a terrible thing to happen.*

When the judge nodded, Rachel cantered a small circle, prepared for the jump and headed for the last two obstacles. Gone was her perfect, quiet horse. Gazelle tossed her head and snorted like a wild thing as she cantered much too fast up to and over the fences. Jessa could see the look of bitter disappointment on Rachel's face. She wondered if Rachel would beat enough other riders in the last class to still have a place in the ribbons in the overall standings. Jessa wiped her palm on her jods. Watching Rachel and Gazelle's round did nothing to boost her confidence.

"That's too bad," said Marjorie who was watching next to Jessa. "That could have happened to anyone. You'd think people would know better than to bring a balloon to a horse show."

Finally, it was Jessa's turn. She gave Rebel a pat on the neck and clucked to him. They circled once at a quiet canter and headed for the first jump.

Rebel hopped over neatly. Three even strides and they took the next fence without any trouble.

Keep your eyes up. Look for the next fence. Steady . . . calm . . . slow. . . .

In her head, Jessa repeated all she had learned from Rebecca. One by one, she and Rebel jumped the fences. As she steered Rebel to the last fence, a small vertical, she was amazed how quickly they had come to the end of the course.

Not too fast . . . approach nice and straight . . . easy. . . .

And they were over!

Jessa walked Rebel through the out-gate and rubbed his neck. She beamed at Cheryl who bounded over to greet them.

"I didn't fall off!" Jessa grinned.

"Of course not! You were great! Rebel was great!"

Two more horses finished their rounds.

Marjorie and Babe entered the ring. Jessa watched closely as they picked up their rocking horse canter and headed for the first fence. It was quickly obvious that the pair was not only good on the flat—they were brilliant over fences.

Babe's rhythm was so steady, so even, she could have been cantering to a metronome. As for Marjorie, she looked totally calm and comfortable from the first fence to the last. Jessa made up her mind to plan her visits to Dark Creek when Marjorie was riding. She could probably learn a thing or two from the older woman and her pretty mare!

After the last rider had left the ring, the steward and the judge consulted. The judge kept pointing at his notes and shaking his head.

"I'm so nervous! What's taking so long?" asked Cheryl, stroking Rebel's soft nose.

Finally, the announcer called out the winners of the third class.

"In first place, Sam Michaels on Beatrice . . . and in second place, Marjorie Hamilton on Toyland Babe. . . ."

Jessa and Cheryl both whooped with delight.

"Go Dark Creek!" screamed Cheryl.

Jessa and Cheryl were still cheering for Marjorie when the third place rider, Allison Raymond, rode in to pick up her ribbon.

". . . in fourth place, Jessa Richardson on Rebel. . . ."

Jessa and Cheryl stared at each other in disbelief. Another ribbon! That was one in each class!

Jessa rode back into the ring. She could hear Cheryl hooting and cheering from behind her.

Jessa claimed her other ribbons from the ring steward and left the ring again to await the final score which would determine the Hunter Classic Champion and the winner of the High Point Trophy.

The judge and one of the stewards pored over their clipboards and compared notes. After what seemed like ages, the judge said something into his walkie-talkie and Mr. Blumen walked into the ring with the trophy and the halter.

"This was a close competition today, ladies and gentlemen," the announcer began. "In reverse order, here are the results. . . . In sixth place with 37 points, Roberta Wilmer. In fifth place, Rachel Blumen and her horse, Gazelle. Bad luck in that last class, Rachel."

Rachel rode into the ring to claim her rosette. She steadfastly ignored her father and looked only at the ring steward who handed her the big, green ribbon.

"Our fourth place winner today will also take home a gift certificate from Oh Suzanna's Tack and Feed Emporium. How about a round of applause for Jessa Richardson who comes in fourth with 39 points—congratulations Jessa and Rebel."

Jessa nearly fell out of her saddle. *Fourth place over all? She had actually beaten Rachel? She couldn't believe it!*

"That's you!" squealed Cheryl. "Go! Go in and get your rosette!"

As if in a haze, Jessa rode back into the ring to where the judge was standing beside Mr. Blumen.

"Congratulations," he said. "You rode very well today."

Jessa looked at the rosette blankly as she realized there was no way she could manage all her ribbons and the gift certificate with her sore wrist.

"Here—I'll take that for her—I'm her trainer."

Jessa laughed as Cheryl came running up to the judge, took the bundle of ribbons and hoisted them high above her head!

Jessa reached forward and patted Rebel on the neck. What a wonderful horse!

She and Cheryl were so busy admiring the fluttering ribbons they didn't hear who had placed third and second. When the announcer paused dramatically before announcing the name of the Champion, they stopped talking to see who would win the big trophy, the cash prize and the fancy leather halter.

"And our Champion today, ladies and gentlemen, is no stranger to the show ring. I see great things ahead for Marjorie Hamilton and her new horse, Toyland Babe!"

"Marjorie! Yay, Marjorie!" shouted Jessa. Marjorie rode in and accepted her trophy from Mr. Blumen. It was too heavy for her to lift high, so she rested it on her thigh. It glinted and shone in the bright sunshine.

Jessa rode to the out-gate of the ring to congratulate her stable-mate. Jeremy trotted past her on Caspian on the way to his next class. He gave her a big smile and a wave as he went by.

"You know who else is really happy?" Cheryl asked.

"Who?" asked Jessa.

"Mrs. Bailey. She was sitting behind us and when she saw you riding she said you were obviously well enough to harvest more horse apples!"

Jessa laughed. Even the thought of cleaning the barn couldn't wipe away her big, happy grin.

Team Trouble at Dark Creek

Mrs. Bailey threatens to sell Dark Creek Stables when a team of huge, clumsy draft horses take up residence and start causing trouble. Then, it starts to snow and just won't stop! What will Jessa do when she and the team have to battle through the blizzard to save a life?

Read about the Christmas vacation Jessa will never forget in *Team Trouble at Dark Creek*, the second book in the StableMates series from Sono Nis Press.

Visit the Dark Creek Website!
http://www.seeknet.com/rebel.htm

About the Author

Nikki Tate's first word wasn't "Ma-Ma"—it was "horsie." She started riding before she started school and has never stopped. She lives in the countryside of southern Vancouver Island and rides regularly with her daughter, Dani.

"Every piece of fiction I write is based on something which really happened. I just wish the piece of reality in this book had nothing to do with a rotten bridge. . . ."